WINGE

Barbara Cartland

Barbara Cartland Ebooks Ltd

This edition © 2018

ISBNs

9781788671392   EPUB

9781788671408   PAPERBACK

Book design by M-Y Books
m-ybooks.co.uk

THE BARBARA CARTLAND ETERNAL COLLECTION

The Barbara Cartland Eternal Collection is the unique opportunity to collect all five hundred of the timeless beautiful romantic novels written by the world's most celebrated and enduring romantic author.

Named the Eternal Collection because Barbara's inspiring stories of pure love, just the same as love itself, the books will be published on the internet at the rate of four titles per month until all five hundred are available.

The Eternal Collection, classic pure romance available worldwide for all time .

THE LATE DAME BARBARA CARTLAND

Barbara Cartland, who sadly died in May 2000 at the grand age of ninety eight, remains one of the world's most famous romantic novelists. With worldwide sales of over one billion, her outstanding 723 books have been translated into thirty six different languages, to be enjoyed by readers of romance globally.

Writing her first book 'Jigsaw' at the age of 21, Barbara became an immediate bestseller. Building upon this initial success, she wrote continuously throughout her life, producing bestsellers for an astonishing 76 years. In addition to Barbara Cartland's legion of fans in the UK and across Europe, her books have always been immensely popular in the USA. In 1976 she achieved the unprecedented feat of having books at numbers 1 & 2 in the prestigious B. Dalton Bookseller bestsellers list.

Although she is often referred to as the 'Queen of Romance', Barbara Cartland also wrote several historical biographies, six autobiographies and numerous theatrical plays as well as books on life, love, health and cookery. Becoming one of Britain's most popular media personalities and dressed in her trademark pink, Barbara spoke on radio and television about social and political issues, as well as making many public appearances.

In 1991 she became a Dame of the Order of the British Empire for her contribution to literature and her work for humanitarian and charitable causes.

Known for her glamour, style, and vitality Barbara Cartland became a legend in her own lifetime. Best remembered for her wonderful romantic novels and loved by millions of readers worldwide, her books remain treasured for their heroic heroes, plucky heroines and traditional values. But above all, it was Barbara Cartland's overriding belief in the positive power of love to help, heal and improve the quality of life for everyone that made her truly unique.

AUTHOR'S NOTE

The first race recorded on Newmarket Heath was in 1622, but it was not until the Restoration in 1660 that Newmarket became the headquarters of British racing.

King Charles II spent a great deal of time in Newmarket and there was a tunnel leading from his Palace (pulled down in Queen Victoria's reign) to Nell Gwynn's house.

The King instituted the Town Place in 1664, but after his death the Race Meetings declined.

But the 'Keeper of the Running Horses' to William and Mary, Queen Anne, George I and George II ruled Newmarket with a rod of iron.

The Jockey Club was formed in Newmarket in 1752, by the well-known patrons of *The Star & Garter* in Pall Mall, began bit by bit, to acquire the Heath and rule the Turf.

CHAPTER ONE
1814

The Earl of Poynton was dining in the style that he was accustomed to.

The ornaments on the table and the plates were of gold, the crystal glasses were engraved with his crest and fruit was in *Sèvres* dishes.

There was no one in the whole of Society, not excluding the Prince Regent, who lived in such grandeur and inevitably such comfort, as the Earl.

In all his houses everything seemed to run with a perfection like himself. He not only had carried on where his father had left off but had also improved his estates until they were spoken of as a fine example to every landowner.

It went without saying that his horses, because he gave them his personal and special attention, were superb.

Although he evoked a certain amount of envy and jealousy, most other sportsmen acknowledged that the Earl deserved the accolades that he won on the Turf year after year.

Sitting at the top of the table, handsome although with a cynical look, distinguished and autocratic, he had an air of authority that made him seem positively majestic.

'Dammit all!' his friend Eddie Lowther thought, 'from the way he looks, and even more from the way he behaves, he might be a King!'

The Earl was entertaining the wealthiest and the most outstanding sport lovers in the country at his house at Newmarket.

Not only because there was to be a Race Meeting there in two days' time but also because they were all interested in a very exceptional sale that was to take place the following day.

"I cannot understand why Melford is selling up his stable," one of the Earl's guests remarked with a puzzled note in his voice. "God knows he is wealthy enough to keep all his horses in comfort and he has been fairly successful in the last two years. Why then should he retire?"

"The answer may be," an elderly man replied before anybody else could speak, "that he has not been in good health lately. He has therefore decided, so I heard, to concentrate on breeding, which he can do much more satisfactorily on his estate in Sussex, instead of braving the bitter winds that we have to endure at Newmarket, and even harsher weather when we visit the Racecourses in the North."

Heads round the table nodded to acknowledge that this might be the reason for Sir Walter Melford's sale and the Earl replied,

"All I can say is that I am glad of the opportunity of adding to my own stable. Melford has some good horses, particularly Raskal and Mandrake."

"Dammit, Poynton," one of the diners exclaimed, "those are the two horses I wanted, but if you are bidding against me I shall not have a chance of acquiring them."

"I don't intend to pay over the odds for them," the Earl replied, "and I think we should keep our heads clear tomorrow because Melford is known to be sharp as a razor when it comes to money."

"That is true." Eddie Lowther nodded. "Personally I have never liked the fellow. He once played a shabby trick on a friend of mine, in fact I might almost say it was crooked."

This time there was a murmur from the other diners and it was quite obvious that Sir Walter Melford was no favourite with any of them.

"Whatever he is like as a person," the Earl remarked, "let's concentrate on his horses, but only pay him what they are worth. If the reserves are too high, leave them well alone."

He spoke in a way that was almost an order and his guests remembered that the Earl was noted as being a hard man but just.

There had been many occasions in the sporting world when he had been exceedingly generous to somebody down on his luck. But he never spoke about them and, because even his closest friends were somewhat in awe of him, they never asked him questions that he would not wish to answer.

Eddie Lowther, who was closer to the Earl than anybody else, was, however, wondering what it was about Sir Walter Melford that, despite his interest in the Turf and despite the excellent horses he ran at most of the classic Race Meetings, had prevented him from being accepted by the elite of the sporting fraternity, which was led by the Earl.

He thought now that he would not be surprised if this was the real reason why Sir Walter was selling his stable.

Although he had made every possible approach, he had never been elected a member of the Jockey Club, just as in some mysterious manner at every attempt he had made to enter White's Club he had been blackballed.

Perhaps Sir Walter was beginning to feel that it was better to be a big fish in a small pond, which he undoubtedly would be in other sporting circles, than a little fish in a big one and in competition with the Earl and his contemporaries.

The rest of the party were having an animated conversation about the other horses that they were interested in acquiring if Raskal and Mandrake were barred as being reserved for the Earl.

"The trouble is, Poynton," one of them said, "that if you are not bidding, we shall all feel suspicious that you know something to their detriment about the animals in question that we don't."

"That is true," another guest agreed. "If anything would make me determined not to put my hand in my pocket, it would be that you thought that those particular horses were not worth the price."

The Earl laughed.

"You are making me feel omnipotent."

"Curse you! That is exactly what you are," was the reply. "You don't suppose that any of us here would challenge you when it came to a knowledge of horseflesh."

"But we will go on trying!" somebody called out.

"Of course you will," the Earl drawled, "and I suppose really I should say modestly that I have just been lucky."

The way he spoke told those who listened all too clearly that he knew that it was nothing of the sort.

It was because he had studied the form of his own horses, superintended the mating of his mares and to all intents and purposes did his own training that he had a knowledge of racing that was unequalled by any other owner in the country.

Eddie gave a laugh and raised his glass.

"To your continued success, Lennox," he said. "And may you reign over us forever even if occasionally we have revolutionary feelings against your sovereignty!"

There was a shout of laughter at this and the Earl was about to reply when a servant came to his side.

"Excuse me, my Lord," he said in a low voice, "there's a young lady at the door who says it's imperative she speaks to your Lordship."

"A young lady?" the Earl questioned. "Is she alone?"

"She's riding, my Lord."

"Tell her if she wants to see me to come back tomorrow morning."

"I've already suggested that, my Lord, but she says she has to see your Lordship immediately and it's a question of life or death."

The Earl raised his eyebrows as if he thought that the servant was being facetious. Then realising that it was his butler who had been with him for many years he asked,

"She is a *lady*, Parker?"

He accentuated the word and the butler replied,

"Undoubtedly, my Lord."

Knowing that Parker could never be deceived in regard to the social status of any man or woman, the Earl said,

"Very well, show her into the Morning Room and tell her to wait."

"I beg your Lordship's pardon, but the young lady asks particularly if you'd come outside to speak with her. I think she wishes, my Lord, to show you her horse."

The Earl frowned as if he felt that he was being pressured and then unexpectedly, because at least this was an unusual situation, he replied,

"Oh, very well, Parker, but I dislike being interrupted during a meal."

"I'm aware of that, my Lord, but the young lady is very persistent."

The Earl pushed back his chair and said to the man next to him,

"I will not be more than a minute or two. Keep the port circulating."

"You can be sure of that," his friend replied.

Without hurrying and with the frown still between his eyes, the Earl walked from the dining room along the richly furnished corridor that led to the hall.

His house was one of the most impressive in Newmarket, and, while he thought of it as a small Racing Lodge, it undoubtedly compared favourably with any ancestral home of the same size elsewhere in the country.

The gardens had been landscaped to relieve the flatness of the ground and the trees planted as a break against the bitter winds that always seemed to be blowing over the Downs.

Although it had been a warm day, it had grown cold in the evening and the Earl thought that might account for the very pale face dominated by two large eyes that was turned towards him as he came down the steps from the front door.

The girl who had asked to see him was small and slender and her hair under the high-crowned riding hat was so fair that for the moment in the dusk the Earl thought that it was white.

Then he realised that she was very young, almost, he thought, immature, but she was undoubtedly a lady and it was surprising that she should have called on him at such an hour without even a groom to accompany her.

He reached her side to say,

"I understand that you wish to speak to me and you have sent a somewhat dramatic message with your request."

"It is – very kind of your Lordship – but I *had* to see you!"

Her voice was low and musical, but there was in the last words a note of desperation that the Earl did not miss.

He stood taking in every detail of her and after a moment, as if she expected him to speak and as he did not do so, was forced to go on,

"Will you please – look at my – horse and then – buy him from me?"

"He is yours to sell?"

"Yes, he is mine – I swear to you – he is mine! But I want you to – have him."

"Why?" the Earl asked perfunctorily.

The girl glanced over her shoulder, almost as if she thought that somebody might be listening, before she answered,

"Perhaps you could inspect Star and if you are – willing to – buy him as I want you to do – then I could explain – where we could not be overheard – why it is necessary."

The Earl was aware that she was speaking about the groom who was standing near the steps, ready to take the horse to the stables if necessary, and of the footmen who had followed him out from the front door and were standing stiffly on either side of it as if waiting for orders.

Without saying anything, the Earl looked at the horse carefully and could see that it was well-bred with a fine head.

It was jet black, the only patch of colour being a white star on its nose and he knew at the first glance that it was a horse he would not be ashamed to have in his stables and that it would undoubtedly prove a good hunter.

Because he took trouble over everything he did, the Earl inspected the horse more closely from the front and the sides and then, patting the animal on the neck, said,

"I imagine your horse is four years old."

"And three months, my Lord."

"You have a record of its breeding?"

"Yes, my Lord. I have written it down."

"Very well, I will now send him to my stables while you come inside and tell me this momentous secret that can only be related in private."

He spoke sarcastically as if he thought that there could be nothing that warranted her intrusion at this particular hour.

The girl put out her hand to touch the horse as if to reassure him and he turned and nuzzled her before at a gesture from the Earl the groom came to his head.

The man led the horse away in the direction of the stables and the girl walked up the steps beside the Earl.

When they reached the hall, he led the way not to the Morning Room, but towards his study where he usually held interviews with anyone who called to see him.

A footman hurriedly opened the door and the Earl walked ahead into the room that was hung with pictures of horses by the greatest artists of the last two hundred years.

He was used to anyone who entered his study for the first time exclaiming in admiration first at the pictures and then at the comfortable way that it was furnished with sofas and chairs in dark red leather.

There was also a desk and other furniture, which were glorious examples of Robert Adam's genius.

But on this occasion the Earl's visitor just stood a little way inside the door looking at him in a manner that he could not help recognising was one of pleading.

"I suggest you sit down," he said "and then quickly, because I am entertaining friends, tell me what all this is about."

"I am – very grateful to you for – seeing me, my Lord."

As the girl spoke, she sat down on the very edge of the armchair that the Earl indicated. She had taken off her riding gloves and he saw, as she linked her fingers together, how nervous she was.

"First before you begin," the Earl said, "I suggest you tell me your name."

"It is Cledra, my Lord. Cledra Melford."

The Earl looked surprised.

"Melford? Are you any relation to Sir Walter Melford, who is holding a sale tomorrow?"

"He is my uncle."

"Your uncle? And yet you are asking me to buy your horse this evening before the sale begins?"

"Star is not to be put in the sale tomorrow, my Lord, so that you or any of your friends could bid for him. He is to be sold – privately to a man who will – ill-treat him.

As if she thought that the Earl looked skeptical, Cledra said hastily,

"It is true! I swear to you, that my uncle is selling Star to a man called Bowbrank – who has a – reputation for – cruelty."

She looked desperately at the Earl as she went on,

"I would rather – kill Star – myself than let – him suffer in such a way."

She thought as she spoke that the Earl looked skeptical, as if he felt that she was being hysterical, but she went on,

"Mr. Bowbrank works his horses so hard that three of them died last year from sheer exhaustion and they are always beaten on every journey because he believes that is the only way that he can get any speed out of them."

"Bowbrank!" the Earl exclaimed. "You mean the man who owns the inn that supplies Post chaises and other vehicles in Newmarket."

"Yes, my Lord, I thought you might have heard of him."

"And you tell me he is cruel to his animals? Surely that would not be a very economical way of running his business?"

"He is cruel not only because he is insensitive but also because he drinks, my Lord."

Again Cledra thought that the Earl was not impressed by what she had said and she begged him,

"Please – please believe me – and Uncle Walter is selling Star to this man simply because he wants to hurt me. He knows that if I think of Star – suffering in such a – way I shall want to – die."

"Why should your uncle wish you to be so unhappy?" the Earl enquired.

"Because he hates me," Cledra replied, "just as he hated my father."

"You speak as if your father is dead."

"Yes – he died four months ago. He and – Mama were killed in an accident and I had to come and live with my uncle as there was – nowhere else for me to go."

The Earl did not speak and after a moment she went on,

"Papa had no money – in fact he was in debt – but Star is mine. He was registered in my name and therefore Uncle Walter could not claim him. But now he says that I am to sell him to pay for my board and keep with him – and, as he is my Guardian – there is nothing I can do to – stop him."

"What you are asking me to do is to buy your horse before he can be handed over to this man Bowbrank."

"Yes, my Lord."

"And give you the money, I suppose?"

"Oh, no, that was something else I was going to ask you," Cledra replied. "When Uncle Walter came and took me away from the house – where I had lived with Papa and Mama in Essex he refused to pension the old maid who had looked after me ever since I was a child – or to give anything to the groom who had cared for Papa's horses and who was almost like one of the family."

There was a sob in her voice as she continued,

"He left them penniless, my Lord, except for the very little money I could give them, which I obtained by selling Mama's jewellery – without Uncle Walter being aware of it."

The Earl looked at Cledra searchingly as if he could hardly believe what she was saying.

Yet the same instinct he relied on when he was looking at a horse told him that what she was saying was the truth.

He was also aware that, as she was speaking, she was straining with every nerve in her body to persuade him to do what she wished.

"It is certainly a very odd request, Miss Melford," he said slowly, "and why, as you have never met me previously, have you come to me instead of to a friend of your father."

"Papa's friends are all in Essex where we lived," Cledra answered, "and it was only yesterday – when I overheard a conversation that I realised what Uncle Walter was – about to do."

She drew in her breath as if in pain and then carried on,

"When I challenged him, he told me that Star was not good enough to be put in the sale with his own horses, but I knew actually it was because he wished to – punish me because I am Papa's daughter."

"It seems a strange reason," the Earl remarked.

"Papa was everything Uncle Walter is not!" Cledra replied. "To begin with he was a real sportsman, kind, understanding and – always ready to help other people. He was a soldier until that became too expensive for him and then he and Mama went to live very quietly in the country. But because everybody who met Papa loved him, he became very popular and – that annoyed Uncle Walter."

Cledra paused and the Earl realised that because she was speaking of her father who had so recently died, she was fighting valiantly against the tears that made her eyes glisten, but which she would not let fall,

"Besides which," she went on, "Papa and Mama were invited to stay with many of the people who would not ask Uncle Walter because they did not like him. They went to balls and were guests at house parties and Race Meetings and because Papa was such good company and because he was fond of him a friend of his made him a member of White's."

The Earl thought that this, if nothing else, would have rankled with Sir Walter who was unacceptable in the smartest and most distinguished Club in St. James's.

After what had been said at dinner, he found himself beginning to believe Cledra's story. Then he thought that, like all women, she was probably exaggerating.

Yet she looked very young and pathetic and was apparently alone in a hostile world in which her only relative disliked her.

After a moment he said slowly,

"What you are asking me to do is to buy Star from you and send the money to two people whom you feel your uncle should have pensioned off after your father's death."

"W-would you do that? Would you – really?"

There was a sudden little lilt in Cledra's voice that had not been there before and her eyes were shining.

"I suppose it is possible for me to do so," the Earl said, "but I think that your uncle would consider it a strange way for me to behave."

Cledra gave a cry that seemed to echo round the room.

"Uncle Walter must never know that you have bought Star – or where he is."

"Do you think that he might take his revenge upon me?" the Earl asked mockingly.

"Oh, no – not on you – but on Star. Last year there was a horse that – died and – "

Cledra stopped suddenly.

"I-I am sorry – I should not have – said that."

"I think that, having started something so momentous, it would be extremely irritating if you did not finish what you were about to say."

"It would be – better for you not – to know."

"But I insist!"

The Earl spoke in a way that would have made it hard for a man, let alone a woman, not to obey him and after a moment Cledra said uncomfortably, as if she was regretting that she had ever brought up the subject,

"Do you remember the Craven Handicap at the Spring Meeting?" she began hesitatingly.

"Yes," the Earl replied.

"It was won – if you remember – by Lord Ludlow with his horse called – Jessop."

The Earl nodded.

"It beat Uncle Walter's horse by a nose."

"Yes, I do recall the race."

"Uncle Walter was very angry. He disliked Lord Ludlow anyway – and, apparently because he only had a few horses and Uncle Walter has a great many, Lord Ludlow rather crowed over him after the race."

"What happened?" the Earl asked.

"Uncle Walter was very very angry that evening and the next day – Jessop was found – dead in his – stall."

The Earl looked at her before he said with a note of incredulity in his voice,

"Are you seriously suggesting that your uncle was responsible for the death of that horse?"

Because he spoke scathingly the colour rose in Cledra's pale cheeks and she looked away from him.

"P-perhaps I should not – have told you – but I overheard by mistake something that he – said to one of the men who works for him – and I know too where he keeps the – poison that was – used in Jessop's water."

It seemed incredible and yet once again the Earl was aware that Cledra was speaking with a sincerity that he could not doubt.

Before he could say anything further she added,

"That would happen to Star – I know it would – and I was going to ask if you buy him from me that you should take him away from here as quickly as – possible and – register him under a different name."

"I find it very hard to credit what you are saying to me," the Earl declared. "You don't think because Star means so much to you that you are perhaps exaggerating the danger he is in?"

"I swear to you that I have not exaggerated or said anything that is not true and I know that, if Uncle Walter becomes aware that I have sold Star to you, he will die or suffer in some – horrible way that I cannot – bear to think about."

"It seems incredible!" the Earl remarked beneath his breath.

"There have been a number of other incidents since I have been living with my uncle in Newmarket but I don't wish to speak about them," Cledra said. "I am concerned only with saving Star and obtaining the money somehow to the two people whom Mama and Papa trusted and who have worked for us ever since I can remember."

The Earl thought that apart from Cledra's story about the death of Jessop the fact that he had left two old servants unprovided for confirmed everything that he had heard about Walter Melford and justified the instinctive dislike that he had always had for him.

While he was thinking it over, he was aware that Cledra was watching his face and the anxiety and fear in her eyes was so expressive that he felt almost as if she was kneeling in front of him and praying that he would do what she asked.

"Would you think," he asked, "that six hundred guineas is a fair price for your horse?"

Cledra gave a little cry.

"You will really give as much as that for him? Oh, thank you – thank you. And thank you for saying you will – have him. I know he will be – safe with you."

"What makes you so sure of that?"

"Papa admired you enormously. He used to follow your successes on the Racecourses and say, 'Poynton has won again. I am so glad, he is a great sportsman and has an unsurpassed knowledge of horses'."

"Thank you," the Earl said with a faint touch of amusement in his voice. "That is the sort of compliment I like to hear."

"Papa was not saying it to you, he was simply stating a fact."

The Earl acknowledged the distinction with a smile and Cledra went on,

"I knew that you were the only person I could really trust with – Star. He is so gentle and so intelligent. He will do anything I ask of him and Papa and I taught him not with a whip – but with – love."

Her voice was very moving and, because what she felt and what she was saying came from her heart, it vibrated in her voice.

"You will miss him," the Earl murmured.

He then saw the expression of pain that crossed her face.

"I shall be – h-happy because he is with – you," she said in a low voice.

The Earl walked towards his desk.

"If you will give me the names of the people who are to receive three hundred guineas each," he said, "I will instruct my secretary to despatch it to them tomorrow morning."

Cledra put her hand into the pocket of her jacket.

"I have it written down together with Star's pedigree. But I am wondering how it could be explained to Martha and Jackson that their money has to be put into a Bank, otherwise it might be stolen."

"I think it would be much simpler," the Earl answered, "for them to go on my roll of pensioners and receive their money every week."

"Would you – really, my Lord?"

"It would not be difficult. I quite understand your anxiety that an old person living alone should not have so much money, which would be a temptation to thieves."

"You are very – understanding."

"I will also instruct one of my senior estate clerks to visit them every so often," the Earl offered, "to see that their cottages are in good repair."

There were tears in Cledra's eyes as she said,

"What can I say? How can I – thank you? I have lain awake night after night – worrying as to whether

Martha – whom Mama loved – was ill or Jackson was starving because he was too old to find work."

"Well, now you can stop worrying. Leave everything to me and try to enjoy yourself."

Cledra did not speak and he had the feeling that it would be impossible for her to do so as long as she lived with her uncle.

Because he did not wish to be involved any more than he was already, the Earl rose from his desk to say,

"Everything is now settled to your satisfaction, but how do you intend to return to your uncle's house?"

"I will walk," Cledra replied. "It is not more than two miles."

"I will send you in one of my carriages."

She shook her head.

"Somebody might see me and Uncle Walter must never, never – know where – Star has – gone."

"He will be quite safe with me," the Earl stated confidently. "As you have asked me to do, I will change his name and tomorrow he will go to my estate in Hertfordshire where he will, I promise you, be well looked after."

"I know that and thank you – thank you for being so very – wonderful."

There was such a depth of gratitude in the way Cledra spoke that for the moment the Earl's hard eyes seemed to soften.

He put out his hand.

"Goodbye, Miss Melford, and, as my guests are waiting for me, you will understand if I don't escort you to the door. I expect too that before you leave you would like to go to the stables and say 'goodbye' to your stallion."

As he took her hand in his, he found that it was very cold and quivering in a way that told him how deeply moved she was by everything that had happened.

Then, when he would have turned away and left her, she bent her head and he felt her lips against his hand.

*

Leaving the stables where she had found Star in a comfortable stall, Cledra felt as if she had left behind the only being in her life that she had to love.

She could not prevent herself from crying as she had kissed Star and he nuzzled against her affectionately.

She knew that he would miss her, but for her the future was empty and dark with misery without even those moments of happiness when she could be with Star and know that he loved her as she loved him.

Ever since her father and mother had been killed and she had come to live with her uncle at Newmarket she had been surrounded by indifference and even hatred.

Both attitudes had eaten into her very soul so that she felt that there were times when she must lose her very identity and no longer be herself.

Because her uncle had no wish for her to meet his friends or even for them to be aware that she was related to him, he had never taken her to London where he had a large house.

Instead she had travelled from Essex to Newmarket to find that his servants were as she might have expected, subservient and frightened of him, but arrogant, aggressive and unpleasant when he was not there.

Because they resented her intrusion, they gave her the minimum service when she was alone and soon learnt that, as her uncle despised her, they could despise her too.

The only way that she could escape from a house that seemed always dark and without sunlight was by riding her own horse.

When her uncle had sold up everything that her father and mother had possessed and not allowed her to keep any of the treasures that she could not prove were her own, the only thing she had left besides her clothes was Star.

She had come with him to Newmarket and at least he had been comfortable in a stable that housed her uncle's horses, although she had never cared for the grooms who looked after them.

She soon learnt the reason why her uncle was dissatisfied with his racehorses.

It was, as Eddie Lowther had shrewdly guessed, because he was not accepted as a member of the Jockey Club and therefore always felt inferior on every Racecourse.

There were plenty of other owners who were only too willing, because he was so wealthy, to be friendly with him, but Sir Walter was ambitious.

He had expected, because he had made himself a great fortune, to be able to buy the best of everything, including the membership of fashionable Clubs.

He was therefore infuriated when he found that it was impossible.

He had made his money in various reprehensible ways including, Cledra's father had once told her, by cheating several foolish and trustful young men out of their inheritance before they were old enough to understand what he was doing.

He had also been engaged in various nefarious deals on the Stock Exchange and when he gambled it was always on a certainty, which was not considered a sporting gesture.

But while he was rich and his brother was poor, George and his wife were friends with people who would not speak to Walter Melford and stayed in houses that would not have allowed him in even through the servants' entrance.

Cledra had often heard her father say laughingly to her mother,

"We may be poor, darling, but we are rich in friendship and, of course, love."

He had kissed his wife as he spoke who had replied in her daughter's hearing,

"If love counts, then I am richer than the Queen of Sheba and very very much happier!"

Her father had laughed and Cledra had felt that the whole house where they lived was always filled with sunshine and their happiness radiated out to everyone who knew them.

It was only when her parents died that she understood how much Sir Walter had loathed his younger brother simply because he was jealous of him.

She soon learnt that the years of frustration could somehow be recompensed if he could torture her and feel that he was getting his own back because she was her father's daughter.

At first he only jeered at her, sneered at her father's poverty and disparaged her mother.

Then when she defied him and defended them he had first slapped her and then beat her.

She knew the first time he did so that he had enjoyed it and would do it again.

Any excuse after that made him bring out the wiry little whip that he used on his horses and his dogs and she went in terror lest he should beat Star.

It was not difficult for him to learn that to Cledra his treatment of her horse was far more painful than any physical punishment on her.

Once or twice when he had ordered that the horse should not be fed for twenty-four hours, he delighted in watching her suffering as he reiterated that periods of starvation were good for both men and beast.

"But animals don't – understand why they are – treated in that way, Uncle Walter," Cledra had said tremulously.

"Then your horse will learn, my dear, and doubtless will be grateful when tomorrow or the next day his feeding is resumed."

That night, when she thought that her uncle was asleep, Cledra had attempted to go downstairs intending to creep to the stables to feed Star herself.

But Sir Walter was lying in wait for her and, having beaten her, he locked her in her room and she heard him laughing as he went down the passage.

She told herself then not only that she hated him but he was mad. But it was difficult to know what she could do about it and how she could escape.

There was no one she could turn to for assistance because, even if she ran away to her parents' friends in Essex, she was quite certain that, as her uncle was legally her Guardian, he would fetch her back and be within the law in doing so.

It was only when she heard him arranging to sell Star to the innkeeper, whose name was a byword in Newmarket for the way that he ill-treated his horses that she knew that somehow she must save the animal she loved.

How could she live knowing that he was being whipped and badly treated?

She thought first that the only way she could free him would be to kill him, but she knew that when the moment came she would not be able to pull the trigger.

It was then, almost like a light in the darkness, she thought of the Earl.

Because he was such a renowned sportsman, she thought that he would understand as no one else would how it was impossible to let her horse suffer.

It was her uncle who had inadvertently told her that the Earl was coming to the sale.

"That stuck-up swine, Poynton," he had fumed, talking more to himself than to her, "who will not know me when we meet on the Racecourse, but he will turn up at my sale, make no mistake about that."

Cledra had drawn in her breath.

"Do you mean he will come to Newmarket especially for the sale?" she had asked.

"He will come to Newmarket for the Race Meeting, you idiot!" Sir Walter had snarled. "That is when I am going to have my sale. I am not a fool, for I know that all the top owners at Newmarket will be unable to resist a sale of the finest horseflesh any of them are likely to see."

Cledra wanted to argue that the Earl's horses must be finer than her uncle's since he always won the races when Sir Walter ran against him.

But she knew that such a remark like that would only make her uncle beat her and she therefore remained silent.

"I will make sure that there is plenty of champagne. That always makes the bids go higher," Sir Walter commented, "and I will serve the best dishes my chef can provide. Make no mistake, if I have to give up racing, then I will give it up in style!"

"Why must you give it up?" Cledra asked.

"If you want the truth, because I am fed up with Poynton always passing the Winning Post ahead of me," her uncle shouted. "*Curse him*, but he has the Devil's own luck! I will not watch any more of my money disappearing down an inexhaustible drain and be sniggered at by snobs who will not make me a member of the Jockey Club."

His voice rose louder as he yelled,

"*Blast them*! I will get my own back. You mark my words, I will get all my own back!"

For the last three days he had talked in the same strain over and over again and Cledra felt, although she knew that she dared not say so, that he was growing madder and madder.

At times he would be shrewd and penny-pinching if it concerned spending money on something that he was not interested in.

She had found out since coming to live with him that, while he paid his grooms well, he was miserly over the wages of the older indoor servants who if he dismissed them would be unable to find other employment.

Those who were pensioned off, including the jockeys who had brought him in hundreds of pounds in racing prizes during their day, were almost starving, in the cottages where the roofs leaked and the floorboards were rotting away unrepaired.

When Cledra was alone at Newmarket, she would go and call on the old people.

They told her that they were often hungry, but if they complained in any way were told they could get out and find somewhere else to live.

She knew how horrified her father would have been at his brother's behaviour and how deeply it would distress her mother, but there was nothing she could do except take them fruit from the garden when the gardeners were not looking and hope that her prayers would be answered and something would be done for them.

Sometimes at night she talked aloud to her father and told him how unhappy she was.

"Help me, Papa, help me not only by preventing Uncle Walter from beating me but also by showing me what I can do for the poor old people whom he neglects so viciously."

It was when she learnt of her uncle's plans for Star that she had cried to her father in distress, feeling that he must hear her and somehow by a miracle he would save the horse he had loved as she did,

"Star will never understand why I abandoned him or why he is beaten instead of being loved, Papa. Oh, Papa, tell me what to do! You must help me – *you must.*"

She felt as if her whole being reached out towards her father.

Then, almost like an answer coming from beyond the grave, she knew what she must do.

It was as if her father had said to her,

,Go to the Earl of Poynton. He will buy Star from you and then the money can go to Martha and Jackson.'

It had seemed such a simple solution that Cledra wondered why she had not thought of it herself and, walking back to her uncle's house by the light of the stars, she was saying over and over again in her heart,

'Thank You, God – for letting me hear Papa – and for giving me – the answer. Thank You! *Thank You*!'

CHAPTER TWO

When Cledra had left him to go to the stables, the Earl walked back into the dining room and, as he took his place at the head of the table, one of his guests remarked,

"She must have been pretty, Poynton, to have kept you so long!"

The Earl did not reply and Eddie Lowther was aware that his lips tightened slightly.

It was one of his unbreakable rules that he never at any time discussed the women in his life nor allowed anybody else to do so.

There had been actually a great many of them and Eddie often thought wryly that they were magnetised not only by his position, his wealth and his attractions, which were considerable, but also by the fact that the Earl was elusive and, when it concerned a love affair, extremely unpredictable.

"Has there ever been a woman who did not feel that she could climb the highest mountain when everyone else has failed?" someone had asked once.

It was certainly true where the Earl was concerned.

Unfortunately from the gossips' point of view, his *affaires de cœur*, because he was as fastidious over his women as he was over everything else, were always with ladies who were discreet, reserved and, it went without saying, exceedingly beautiful.

Only Eddie because he was so close to the Earl was aware of how many broken hearts he left behind him.

The loveliest women in the *Beau Monde* wept helplessly into their pillows when they realised that he was now bored with them and they would never see him again except in a crowded ballroom or at a large dinner party.

At the moment the Earl was just coming to the end of what had been an amusing, tempestuous and rather intriguing affair with an ambitious Politician's wife.

She was very lovely, half-Hungarian by extraction and had all the fire in her temperament and in her lovemaking that was denoted by the colour of her hair.

As her husband was kept continually at the House of Commons, the Earl had been able to spend more time with her than was usual.

It was only when he was leaving London for Newmarket that he thought it had been a mistake that they had seen each other so frequently.

He was beginning to know beforehand, which was fatal, exactly what she would say and there had undoubtedly been moments when they were together when he found his thoughts wandering.

What was more, if he was honest, he found now that her continual efforts to arouse his desire was becoming a bore.

While driving down to Newcastle his famous team of perfectly matched chestnuts, which reminded him of her hair, he decided that the affair was at an end. He would send her an expensive present and ring down the curtain on what had been a pleasant interlude, but no more.

With the present would be enclosed a note telling her that it was 'a keepsake', which he hoped would remind her of the many happy hours that they had spent together.

This was almost a routine phrase in his farewell letters, but to the women who received one it was the sound of doom, for they that knew no tears or pleading would have any effect on him.

The strange thing about the Earl was that, unlike most men, he never had to endure recriminations or suffer from women who wished to be revenged because he had left them.

Invariably the recipients of his favours were so grateful that they just cried despairingly.

They also felt that, although he had now closed the gates of Paradise, the ecstasy that they had enjoyed was worth the suffering they now endured.

As he sat down in his high-backed chair, the Earl lifted his glass of port to his lips, ignoring the remark of his guest, which he thought in poor taste.

"Do you wish to play *écarté* after dinner, Lionel," he asked the man gentle next to him. "Or would you prefer *faro*?"

This immediately started an argument as to which was the most enjoyable game of chance and, when the Earl rose to take his guests into the drawing room, there was no other questions regarding his reason for leaving them during the meal.

It was not until several hours later when he was alone in the large comfortable bed with the Poynton Coat of Arms embroidered above the headboard that the Earl found himself thinking of Cledra and the strange story that she had told him about Sir Walter Melford.

He had thought it over for some time before he fell asleep and in the morning when his valet was dressing him he said,

"While I am at the sale today, Yates, find out anything you can about a man named Bowbrank who keeps an inn in Newmarket. I think it is called *The Crown and Anchor.*

"That's right, my Lord."

"You know it?"

"Yes, my Lord, and he be a nasty piece of work. There's tales about him your Lordship wouldn't care to hear."

"Which means, I suppose," the Earl said slowly, "that he is cruel to his horses that he hires out."

"His horses and the lads what looks after them, my Lord."

This confirmed what Cledra had told him for the Earl knew that any information that Yates gave him was always reliable.

A thin, wiry little man, only two years older than the Earl himself, Yates had been his first valet when he left his Public School and went up to Oxford University.

All the 'Top Bloods', which meant the rich undergraduates, had their own valets and their own grooms and it went without saying that Viscount Poyle, as he was then, had the swiftest horses and his phaeton was the smartest in the City.

Yates acquired much reflected glory amongst the other servants because of his Master's outstanding athletic achievements and the way he rode his horses to victory in every Steeplechase that took place at the University.

After Oxford he had gone into the Army and took Yates with him and here again the Viscount distinguished himself.

When fourteen years ago the French Revolution and four years later the Terror, astounded the whole civilised world, Viscount Poyle and his valet were successful in organising the escape of a number of aristocrats from France to the safe shores of England.

The Earl had never talked about these exploits and nor had Yates, but those whom he saved spoke so gratefully and movingly of his brilliance in saving them from the guillotine that the Viscount added another laurel wreath to the many he had accumulated already.

When his father died and he inherited the Earldom, he bought himself out of the Army and settled down to run his estates and concentrate on his horses.

He was well aware that Yates, who had an adventurous nature, often sighed for the excitement and danger of war and he was not surprised when his valet offered eagerly,

"I'll have a sniff around, my Lord, and see what else I can find out about this man, Bowbrank."

"You do that, Yates, and also if the opportunity arises talk to Lord Ludlow's grooms. He is certain to be running a horse at this Meeting. See if they have anything to tell you about the death at the last meeting of Jessop."

The Earl knew by the expression on Yates's face that he not only absorbed everything he said to him but was eager for the excitement of what he called 'spying out the land'.

The Earl had never embarked on any of their daring attempts to rescue aristocrats from France without first making sure that he knew every inch of their hiding place or prison before he went into action.

"Carelessness accounts for more dead men than bullets do," the Earl often commented.

Yates, who had worked so closely with him, knew that this was true.

When the Earl went downstairs for breakfast and afterwards climbed into his phaeton that was waiting outside, he had dismissed from his mind everything that Cledra had told him and was concentrating on the horses that he would like to buy at the sale.

Travelling with him, Eddie Lowther thought that nothing could be smarter or more impressive than the Earl's turnout.

His groom sitting up behind wore a cockaded tall hat and his horses' harnesses was embellished with silver and engraved with the Poynton crest.

The other guests followed in their own vehicles or those provided by the Earl and it was only a short distance to Sir Walter Melford's stables.

These lay behind a gaunt-looking grey stone house that he had purchased some fifteen years earlier when he had first started to race at Newmarket.

There was a faint smile on the Earl's rather hard mouth when he and Eddie were not only greeted effusively by their host but were also pressed to partake of champagne, brandy or any other drink before they had a chance to inspect the horses in the sale.

There were also tables laden with delicacies of every sort including oysters, *pâtés* and a boar's head and a suckling pig.

The Earl, to Sir Walter's consternation, refused any refreshment and Eddie sipped his glass of champagne slowly, remembering how he had been warned the previous evening to keep a clear head.

It was the first time that the Earl and most of his friends had ever been inside Sir Walter's house and they looked somewhat sceptically at the luxury that it was furnished with and the fine pictures that hung on the walls.

When they had been joined by almost every racehorse owner who was at Newmarket, the Earl found himself wondering if he would see Cledra.

He was well aware that if he did so he must pretend not to have met her before, but there being no other ladies present and he guessed that she had been told to keep out of sight.

So he would not see her large eyes, which he remembered looking at him at first pleadingly and then with a gratitude that was rather moving.

When it was getting on for noon and quite a considerable amount of food and wine had been consumed, Sir Walter led the way to the yard at the back of the house where seats had been arranged around a roughly constructed ring.

An auctioneer, whom the Earl knew well from previous sales that he had attended, took over the rostrum and the bidding was brisk from the moment the first horse was led in.

The Earl's guests did not have it all their own way for there was a large number of bidders who had come from all over the country since the sale had been well advertised.

The bids began to go higher and higher and the Earl thought cynically that the money which Sir Walter had expended on refreshments was certainly proving its worth.

There was also a bar erected at the side of the yard where more champagne was provided for anybody who felt the need of it and there was no doubt that, such generous hospitality being unusual, it was fully appreciated by quite a number of those present.

Eddie, who was sitting beside the Earl, said,

"If the bidding for this horse goes over one thousand guineas, it is beyond my purse!"

"I should leave it alone," the Earl suggested, "and, if you want Raskal or Mandrake, they are yours."

"You are not going to bid for them?"

The Earl shook his head.

"Why not?"

"I have no wish for my good guineas to go into that man's pocket."

Eddie looked at the Earl in astonishment, but he had no intention of elaborating further.

Instead he rose to his feet to walk across the yard and into the stable from which the horses had not yet been taken into the ring.

Sir Walter's horses were stabled on both sides of the yard and the auction had started with the horses in the stalls on the left hand side.

There was now a pause before the grooms began to bring into the ring those from the right hand side.

Before the sale started the stables had been so crowded that the Earl had made no effort to inspect the horses.

Now the prospective buyers had apparently seen all that they wanted to see and were engaged in bidding or drinking, which left the stables comparatively empty.

The Earl inspected the horses one by one and found that they were well-bred and most of them in the peak of condition.

But remembering what Cledra had told him, he had the feeling that a number of them seemed restless and timid.

It was hard to believe that Sir Walter could be so foolish as to ill-treat his own horses and yet, if a man would deliberately starve a horse, he would also, the Earl reflected, treat them unnecessarily harshly.

He walked from stall to stall and knew as he did so that the bidding had started again and now the horses he had already inspected were being taken out into the ring.

The stable was a long one, built in much the same manner as his own with wooden partitions between each stall and iron bars above them.

He did not attempt to open the doors of any of the stalls, but looked through the bars at the horses seeing all he wished to see, knowing that he had decided to add none of them to his own stable.

He came to the end and saw that the last stall of about thirty had its iron bars covered with horse blankets, which were tied down so securely that it was impossible to see inside.

He vaguely wondered the reason for this and was just about to turn away when he saw painted on the door of the stall, as all the others, was the horse's name.

It was almost covered by horse-cloths, but he could read the one word, 'Star'.

The Earl stared at it and as he did so a respectful voice behind him came,

"This stall's empty, my Lord, but perhaps your Lordship'd like to see some of the other horses afore they goes into the ring?"

"No," the Earl replied. "I am not interested."

He walked away and the groom hurried to ask the same question of another visitor, obviously hoping for a tip for his pains.

The Earl was silent on the drive home, while Eddie talked about the sale and the astronomical sums that Sir Walter had obtained for his horses.

"He certainly made sure that the bidders were in the right mood," he commented, "and the food was better than we could have found in White's or any other Club in London."

The Earl did not reply and Eddie went on,

"Now I think of it, you drank nothing and ate nothing, Lennox. Why?"

"You may think it old-fashioned of me," the Earl replied, "but I do *not* take his salt or accept the hospitality of any man if I dislike him."

"Why have you suddenly such an aversion to Sir Walter?" Eddie enquired.

He realised that the Earl's voice had been more positive than his usual indifference in speaking of anybody who he had no wish to be acquainted with.

The Earl did not reply and Eddie asked mockingly,

"Are you using your instinct again, Lennox?"

He often teased the Earl because, when they had been in the Army together and spent three years in India fighting under Colonel Arthur Wellesley, his friend's instinct had been respected not only by the troops he commanded but also by his brother Officers.

On more than one occasion he had saved them from walking into an ambush and on another he had sensed that they might be murdered by marauding tribesmen.

Because the Viscount, as he was then, had smelt danger and warned them, they were prepared for the onslaught.

"Perhaps that is the answer," the Earl responded evasively, "but for the moment I don't know."

"I think we have seen the last of Melford," Eddie suggested.

"He has put paid to his aspirations to shine on the Turf as an owner and, when he retires to Sussex, we shall not hear of him again."

"I hope you are right."

Eddie glanced at the Earl and had the feeling that he was hiding something from him.

"What do you know about Melford that you did not know when we were talking about him at dinner last night?" he asked.

The Earl would not be drawn.

"I am not admitting that I know anything more about him. I just don't wish to have horses that have belonged to him in my stable or to accept any hospitality that I have no intention of returning."

"Well, if Melford was rich before, he will be a damned sight richer tonight," Eddie remarked.

The Earl's guests as they drove back said the same thing.

"I paid too much for the horses I bought," one Peer complained, "and I wish to God now that I had left them alone."

"I warned you to keep a clear head," the Earl said.

"I meant, to," the Peer answered, "but the brandy was the best I have tasted for a long time and although I hate to admit it, it made me reckless. *Damn the man*! I wish I had listened to you, Poynton."

"One can hardly blame Melford for getting the best price he could for his animals," another guest remarked, "and personally I am very pleased with my buy. When I win the Gold Cup with him at Ascot, you will all be jealous!"

"So will Melford!" someone exclaimed and they laughed.

After a superlative meal, such as anybody would expect at the Earl's house, they repaired to the drawing room where tables had been laid out for games of chance.

Tonight the party was larger than usual because the Earl had invited a number of his friends from neighbouring estates.

However, as they were all racing the following day, they left at about midnight saying how much they had enjoyed the evening.

"I suppose, Poynton, you will carry off all the prizes tomorrow as you always do," one guest declared philosophically.

"I hope so," the Earl answered, "but an outsider often creeps in when one least expects it."

"I can only pray that it is my horse," somebody answered, "but my prayers have a tiresome way of getting lost on their way to the Winning Post!"

"You should pray harder," the Earl replied.

The guests in the house party did not linger downstairs for long.

"I am going to bed," one of them a little older than the rest announced. "It has been a long day and a very enjoyable one and I need not say, Poynton, that as usual you are the perfect host."

The Earl smiled at the compliment and Eddie noticed that he had not sat down after saying 'goodnight' to his dinner guests in the hall and was obviously hoping that his house guests would soon retire to bed.

It was almost as if they obeyed him without his having to say anything.

Ten minutes later the Earl entered his bedroom where Yates was waiting for him.

"Is everything ready?" he asked.

"The carriage be at the side door, my Lord, where no one'll see it."

"Good," the Earl replied. "Is Hart driving it?"

"Yes, my Lord."

The Earl pulled off his tight-fitting coat and white cravat, which had been intricately tied in the latest style that had received the approval of the great Beau Brummel.

In its place Yates handed him a black silk scarf, which he tied around his neck and fastened in a knot at his throat.

The ends hung over his white shirt and the coat, into which his valet helped him and then covered the rest with a light cloak over his shoulders. He was now dressed entirely in black.

"You have the lantern?" the Earl asked.

"Yes, my Lord, the small one we've used in the past."

"Good."

Yates opened the bedroom door and looked down the passage to see that no one was there. Then he stood back for the Earl to pass him.

Without speaking they walked not along the passage and down the main staircase but to another that led to a door that was seldom opened.

It was at the side of the house where there were few windows and those there did not belong to the principal bedrooms.

The carriage waiting for them was closed and very unobtrusive, being without the Earl's Coat of-Arms on the door or any other means of identification.

It was in fact so ancient that the Earl could not remember when he had last seen it in use.

It was drawn by two horses and the coachman on the box was not wearing the tall cockaded hat or the many-tiered driving coat that he usually wore. Instead he seemed as anonymous as the vehicle he was driving.

The Earl stepped inside, Yates swung himself up on to the box beside the coachman and they moved away.

It was only a short distance to where the carriage came to a stop and the Earl and Yates alighted.

It was a warm night with stars and a moon that was gradually climbing up the sky.

At the same time it was not too brilliant to be embarrassing for anybody who had no wish to be seen.

The carriage had stopped in the shadow of some trees and beside an iron fence that bordered a paddock.

At the far end of it, it was just possible to see the roofs and the upper story of Sir Walter Melford's house.

Without speaking the Earl followed by Yates climbed the fence and moved through the paddock, keeping to the shadows of the trees.

When they came to an open space, they crossed it quickly and waited for a second or so to make sure that nobody watching could have seen them before they moved on again.

At the end of the paddock there was the back wall of the stables and the Earl moved along it until he came to a door at the far end.

Here he paused and waited while Yates crouched down to light the small candle lantern that he had brought with him.

It was specially constructed so that on three sides there were shutters obscuring the light, and it could therefore be directed to illuminate only what was required and not shine indiscriminately.

When the lantern was lit, Yates shone it on the door into the stables, which was fastened with a latch.

The Earl lifted it very slowly and gently without a sound and found that the door was not locked.

He pulled it open and saw ahead, as he had expected, a narrow passage that led directly into the stables, on one side of which there was the stall that he had noted earlier in the day marked with the name 'Star'.

The iron railings at the top of it were still completely covered with horse blankets.

Walking so quietly that it was impossible to hear the sound of his feet, the Earl moved along the narrow passage to the entrance to the stall.

Everything was very quiet except for the movements in some of the further stalls of horses that had been sold earlier in the day, but had not yet been collected by their new owners.

There was no sign or sound of any grooms.

As the Earl had anticipated, by this time they were sleeping off the ale that they had celebrated the success of the sale with and the amount of tips that they had received from the buyers.

He had been aware when he saw the stables that the younger lads would sleep in the loft above them while the older ones would have rooms in another building.

Now he took a special implement from his pocket that he had found of great use in the past.

It certainly made short work of the padlock and when it opened the Earl removed it gently and set it down on the ground before he pushed the door of the stall.

For the moment there was only darkness and the smell of horseflesh and hay until Yates followed him with the lantern.

He directed the light towards the manger and then upwards to the hayloft above it before he turned it downwards and drew his breath.

The Earl had stood still, but now the light shone on a body lying on the floor and he moved forward as if this was what he had expected.

Yates followed him and now the light was on a woman's bare back that was criss-crossed with weals clotted with dried blood.

She was lying face down on a pile of straw and her hands were bound together and were attached by a rope to the bottom of the manger.

Her ankles were also bound and, as the Earl knelt down beside Cledra, he saw that there was a gag in her mouth that was tied tightly at the back of her head.

Taking a knife from his pocket he cut the rope that held her bound hands turned upwards towards the manger and knew, as they fell limply onto the straw, that she was unconscious.

He picked her up in his arms and carried her towards the door followed by Yates.

As he stopped outside it, he waited and without being told Yates knew that he was to close the door and replace the padlock in its original position.

It took only a few seconds before Yates led the way to open the door into the paddock and the Earl came slowly after him, being careful not to knock Cledra's feet against the side of the stall or the passage wall.

When they were outside in the crisp night air. the Earl, who was carrying Cledra so that he touched as little as possible of her bare back, spoke for the first time,

"My cloak!"

Yates lifted it from his shoulders and put it very gently over Cledra.

Then they were moving again, the Earl walking quickly and purposefully towards the fence.

It would have been difficult for anybody watching him to imagine that he carried a half-naked woman in his arms, covered by his dark cloak.

With Yates's help he had no difficulty in lifting Cledra over the iron fence.

When he had placed her on the back seat of the carriage, Yates climbed onto the box, Hart whipped up the horses and they were driving swiftly back the way they had come.

There was nobody about on the empty roads to notice the carriage turning into the Earl's drive and the windows in the house were dark while guests and servants slept peacefully after what had been a long and busy day.

They went in through the side door, the Earl carrying Cledra up the staircase and there was nobody in the passage where his bedroom was situated.

He carried her into his own room and then across it to a door that communicated with a small dressing room, which was filled almost entirely with the wardrobes that contained his clothes.

There was, however, a single bed at one end that was seldom used except as a handy place where Yates laid out the Earl's clothes before he put them on.

Very gently the Earl laid Cledra down on the bed.

He had removed the gag while they were travelling in the carriage, and also cut away the rope that had been tied around her ankles.

She had stirred and, now in the light from the candles that Yates had brought into the room, he looked at her anxiously.

Her face was ashen white, her chest was still, as if she was not breathing and it flashed through his mind that she had been beaten to death or had died of shock from the agony that she must have endured.

He lifted his cloak very slowly from her back aware that the satin lining had stuck in some places to the weals and it would, if she had been aware of it, have hurt her unendurably, as the movement started the blood flowing again.

However she lay completely motionless and now the Earl glanced at Yates who bent forward to feel her pulse.

He was extremely proficient in nursing illnesses and healing wounds.

He had saved the lives of many soldiers in the war by preventing a bayonet thrust or a poisoned sword wound from festering. He has also learned to cope with scorpion and snake bites and fevers that, without his attention, would have proved fatal.

Now for the first time since they had left the paddock, the Earl spoke.

"Is she alive?"

There was a note in his voice that Yates recognised.

He knew better than anybody how angry it had made the Earl when any man under his command had been knifed by an assailant or mutilated after death, as had often happened in India.

"She's alive, my Lord," Yates replied, "but she'll need careful nursin' and her back'll be agony when she's conscious of it."

The Earl looked down at Cledra and appeared to be thinking before he said,

"We have to get her away from here. When will she be well enough to travel?"

"Nobody need know she's here, my Lord. We could move her tomorrow evenin', but it'd be better to wait until the next day."

The Earl nodded.

"I will leave after the second race the day after tomorrow. Nobody will think that in the least strange and I will discuss with you later how best we can take her out of the house without anybody being aware of it. Now you had better do something about her back."

"Leave it to me, my Lord. I've got some salve I'll apply tonight and I'll make somethin' better tomorrow while your Lordship's at the races."

As he spoke, Yates took off Cledra's slippers before he added,

"I'll get the salve and the bandages from my room, my Lord, and then I'll get her into bed."

The Earl nodded again and Yates hurried away, only stopping in the bedroom next door to light some more candles.

The Earl stood very still looking down at Cledra.

In the light from a candelabrum the wounds on her back looked worse than when he had first seen them.

He realised that her uncle must have used a thin, flexible riding whip that had cut sharply into the flesh as effectively as a knife.

The weals crossing and re-crossing each other were deep and the blood from them had run round her body in a crimson stream.

The Earl saw that Sir Walter had torn open the thin muslin gown Cledra had been wearing from the neck to the waist before he had thrown her forward onto the straw in the stall so that he could thrash her more effectively.

It was likely, the Earl thought, that he had gagged her first and to be unable to scream would have made the agony of the beating even more intense than it would otherwise have been.

He wondered how soon it was before she had collapsed into unconsciousness and could only pray that the darkness of oblivion had come quickly before her suffering had become unbearable.

Just as the Earl was appalled at anybody being cruel to an animal, he found it hard to believe that any man with any pretence to humanity could beat in such a bestial manner anything so small and frail as the girl lying on the bed.

He supposed that Sir Walter, having discovered that Star was missing, had taken Cledra to his stall and meted out the punishment that he considered fitted the crime.

It was only by sheer chance that the Earl had been aware that she was there and it was not his intuition in this case that had told him something was amiss when he stood looking at Star's name on the stable door.

Because it puzzled him that horse blankets covered the iron bars at the top of the stall and why the stall itself was padlocked, he had stood silent.

Then he thought that he heard a faint and, as he knew now, muffled whimper. It had been like the sound of a small animal caught in a trap, which ordinarily he would have dismissed from his mind.

It had, however, struck him that it was the sound of something in pain and he had been about to put out his hand to draw aside the horse-cloths to see what lay behind them when the groom had spoken to him and told him that the stall was empty.

Because he was sure that it was a lie, it had made him suspicious and, when he had walked away, he somehow found himself haunted by that whimper of pain.

Travelling home from the sale he had told himself that it was not his business and, if Cledra was right and Sir Walter was cruel to animals, there was nothing he could do about it.

At the same time the whimper kept recurring in his mind until by the time he went up to dress for dinner he knew that it would be impossible for him to sleep unless he found out what had caused it.

It had never struck him for one moment that the sound might have come from Sir Walter's niece.

He had merely imagined after what Cledra had told him that it was a dog that had been shut up in the stable and perhaps beaten for some offence.

Alternatively it might have been another horse he intended to poison as he had allegedly poisoned Lord Ludlow's.

But whatever was inside the locked and shrouded stable, it was something that Sir Walter did not wish anybody to see or know about.

That in itself was enough to make the Earl curious to the point where he knew that he had to rescue whatever was suffering.

Ever since he had rescued aristocrats during the French Revolution he had never undertaken a task without first seeing the layout of the land.

So he had, before he left Sir Walter's sale, deliberately walked to the end of the stable to note the door at the far end and the paddock adjoining it that bordered the road.

Still there was no positive plan in his mind and he kept telling himself that it was wrong for him to embroil himself in any way with Sir Walter.

He had done enough already in buying a horse from his niece.

Then his instinct had come into play and it had told him this was something he had to do for whatever was behind those horse blankets was in considerable pain through cruelty and it was something that he could not ignore.

Now, as he looked down at Cledra's back, he knew that somehow, whatever the consequences to himself, he would protect her from the man who had ill-treated her so brutally and callously.

CHAPTER THREE

The Earl watched his horse win the second race with some ease and received the congratulations of his friends in the Jockey Club box.

He said 'goodbye' to those who had stayed with him for the Meeting and Eddie walked with him to where his phaeton was waiting,

"You are leaving unusually early, Lennox," he remarked.

"I want to be home before it's dark," the Earl replied. "Look after my guests for me and I will meet you in London tomorrow. I shall not be there until late as there are one or two things I have to see to on the estate."

He spoke in his dry, rather bored voice, but Eddie saw that there was an unusual alertness in his bearing and a glint of excitement in his eyes that he had not seen since they had fought together in India.

"I have a feeling, Lennox," he said slowly, "that you are up to something. I have no idea what it can be, but I know you too well to be deceived by your air of indifference."

He wondered as he spoke if there was a new woman. Although he had become aware that the Earl was becoming bored with the Politician's wife, he could not think of anyone who was likely to take her place immediately.

The Earl did not reply to his challenge. He merely smiled enigmatically as he said,

"We will meet in London tomorrow evening and, if you wish to interrogate me, I will invite you to dinner and nobody else."

"So you admit that there is something to interrogate you about?" Eddie persisted.

"I am admitting nothing, except that I dislike people who are inquisitive."

Eddie knew that this was true, but because the Earl was smiling he realised that it was not a put down, such as he would have given to anybody else, and they were too close as friends for him not to be interested.

There was a crowd around the Earl's smart phaeton, which was as well-known as his racing colours were on every Racecourse.

When he swung himself into the driver's seat and picked up the reins, a cheer went up which he acknowledged by raising his tall hat.

Then the phaeton moved off, the crowd scattered in front of the horses, but the cheers continued until it was almost out of sight.

Eddie watched until there was nothing more than a cloud of dust in the distance, then, as he turned back towards the Jockey Club box, it struck him that something was different in the Earl's entourage from usual.

It took him a minute or two to decide what this might be and then he realised that two things were strange, first, the Earl was not accompanied by his usual groom but by Yates and secondly it was unlike him to travel such a distance without outriders.

'Perhaps he will pick them up at the Lodge,' he ruminated.

But the Earl had said distinctly earlier in the morning that he was driving straight from the races to his house in Hertfordshire and was not returning to the Lodge.

'Strange,' Eddie thought to himself and was even more certain than he had been before that something was up.

The Earl in fact was driving as quickly as he could from the Racecourse towards the main highway.

When he turned onto it, he said over his shoulder to Yates who was sitting in the seat behind him,

"Where do we stop?"

"By them trees about fifty yards from here, my Lord. If your Lordship drives into the middle of them, we'll be out of sight of anyone passin' on the road."

The Earl saw the trees a minute or so later and, turning his horses up a cart track, drove slowly and carefully into the middle of the copse.

Here there was a clearing made by woodcutters and Yates jumped down and, moving between the trees, sought something that he had hidden earlier in the day at their foot.

Two seconds later he came back towards the phaeton carrying in his arms a huge wicker basket.

It was what the Earl knew that the gardeners in his various houses used to bring in the fruit and vegetables to the kitchens and inevitably, because there were so many people to feed, a great number were required.

The baskets were not normally as long as the one that Yates was carrying, but he managed extremely skillfully to join two together so that it was now the size of a small coffin.

He carried it to the phaeton and the Earl reached down to help him place it on the floor at his feet.

Between them they wedged it skilfully so that it could not move however fast the horses travelled, and when it was in place the Earl lifted the corner of the light veil of butter muslin that covered Cledra's face.

She was still unconscious, as she had been when he brought her from her uncle's stable to his own house.

But now he was aware that she was breathing naturally and she was in fact sleeping from the herbs that Yates had given her.

Yates had a great knowledge of country herbs, which he had learnt as a boy from his mother, who had been considered a white witch because she could heal local diseases better than any physician.

The first night Cledra's breathing had been so shallow as to be almost indiscernible and the Earl, when he looked at her the following morning, had still been afraid that she might die from the terrible beating that she had received.

But Yates had treated her with his own special skills to bring her back to health.

The Earl had impressed upon him that nobody else in the house must be aware that Cledra was there.

"Don't you worry, my Lord," Yates had answered. "I've already said downstairs that I'm clearin' out your Lordship's wardrobes of a lot of things you've no further use for. They'll therefore be expectin' me to be workin' upstairs."

In case the Earl was not completely satisfied that secrecy would be observed he added,

"I'll keep the doors locked and make sure the housemaids don't see anythin' when they does your Lordship's bedroom. If they hears nothin' and sees nothin', they knows nothin'!"

The Earl nodded.

"That is what I want, Yates."

"I've been thinkin' it over, my Lord," Yates continued, "that it'd be best for the young lady not to realise what's happened to her. She'll be in agony if she comes round, so to speak, so I'll just keep her sleepin' 'till we gets her home."

"That is a good idea," the Earl agreed.

He knew only too well how efficacious Yates's sleeping herbs, which he mixed with honey, could be because he had occasionally drunk them himself.

Once when he was suffering from a high fever that made him so violent that it was impossible for anybody to keep him in bed and on another occasion when a wound that he had received gave him such agony that even with his iron self-control it was hard to stop himself from screaming.

"For God's sake, Yates," he had said then, "give me something to stop this pain. It's driving me mad!"

Yates's herbal draught had not only relieved the pain but also sent him to sleep for nearly twenty-four hours.

Afterwards, although he disapproved of drugs in general, he recognised that it was the best thing that could have happened to him and apart from a very slight headache there had been no after effects.

What was more the wound had healed more quickly than anybody might have expected it to do.

When he stared down at Cledra now, he saw that the ashen whiteness had gone from her face and instead her skin looked translucent.

He thought actually she looked like a Fairy child who might have lived under the trees from which Yates had just brought her.

She was wearing one of his silk nightshirts and her fair hair, as it fell over her shoulders onto the pillow that she was lying on, was longer than he had expected.

Because her knees were bent so that the basket did not have to be longer than was absolutely necessary, she seemed to be cuddled down under the blanket that covered her.

She might, the Earl thought, be sleeping among the flowers of Mount Olympus, where there were no mortals who would ill-treat anyone so young and so exquisite.

Yates broke in on his thoughts.

"She'll be all right, my Lord," he said briskly, "but I'd like your Lordship to drive on and get away from here as quick as possible."

The Earl knew that this was wise advice and he dropped the butter muslin back into place over Cledra's face and Yates tucked it in so that it would not move in the wind.

Then, as he jumped up behind, the Earl turned his team with considerable expertise in such a confined space and drove back onto the highway.

He also wished to go away from Newmarket as quickly as his horses would carry him to make quite certain that Sir Walter had no idea that he was in any way involved with Cledra's disappearance.

Because of what he had learned from Yates yesterday morning, he had been aware that, if Sir Walter Melford had the slightest idea that he was involved in Star's escape from his tyranny and then Cledra's, his horses if nothing else might be in considerable danger.

Yates's investigation had substantiated everything that Cledra had told him.

"I've made a few enquiries about the innkeeper, Bowbrank, my Lord," Yates had said. "He drinks away his profits and it's a scandal in Newmarket the way he treats his horses."

"How does he do any business if that is the way he behaves?" the Earl asked.

"Nobody decent patronises *The Cross and Anchor*, my Lord. It's known to be a place where the tipsters and bookies who welsh if they lose congregate during Race Meetings."

Yates's voice was scathing as he continued,

"The inn itself is cheap and dirty, but Bowbrank does a certain amount of trade with those passing through the town or who want to get away quick 'cos they've lost money."

It was what the Earl had expected to hear and he enquired,

"Have you had a chance to talk to Lord Ludlow's groom?"

"Yes, my Lord, I found him with some difficulty, but after a couple, of drinks he grew quite chatty."

"What did he tell you?"

"He said, my Lord, there was somethin' ever so queer about Jessop's death. The horse was fightin' fit after the race and all of them was cock-a-hoop when he won, especially havin' beaten Sir Walter Melford's Warrior."

Yates paused for a moment and then he went on,

"Then he tells me, my Lord, that, while they were havin' a bit of a celebration in the stables, they hears a strange noise."

Yates paused again, this time dramatically, as he always enjoyed telling a tale somewhat theatrically.

The Earl did not hurry him, as he was anxious to hear all the details.

"One of the lads exclaimed, 'that be Jessop' and they got up to go to the winner's stall."

"What was happening?"

"They thinks the horse were havin' a fit, my Lord. He appeared to be goin' wild, throwin' himself about and screamin' as if he were human. Then suddenly he collapsed."

The Earl thought that this was consistent with the way that poison would react on a man.

"They does all they could for him, my Lord," Yates went on, "but his breathin' got slower and

~61~

slower and the groom said every muscle in Jessop's body were twitchin' until he died."

"They had no idea what caused this?" the Earl asked.

"Lord Ludlow, when they fetched him from the house thought it must be a fit and the next day when they gets a vet in to look at the dead animal he says the same thing. But the groom I were talkin' to had a different idea."

"What did he think?"

"He said the next mornin' when the carcass had been taken away and he were cleanin' up the stall he found that in his frenzy Jessop had kicked over his bucket of water. Wherever it had spread on the floor of his stall, my Lord, anythin' the water had touched was dead."

"What do you mean by 'anything'?" the Earl asked.

"He said there were three mice, a lot of different insects from the hay and they were all a-lyin' on their backs, as dead as Jessop himself."

"Poisoned!" the Earl muttered under his breath.

"Yes, my Lord, that's what the groom thinks and there was sommat else he tells me."

"What was that?"

"He says the next afternoon he goes back to the stall to finish cleanin' it and he found one of the stable yard cats lying on the floor also dead. A young cat it were too."

"And yet the vet found no sign of poison in the horse's body?"

"I don't suppose he looked very careful-like, my Lord," Yates replied. "The horse were dead and there was nothin' he could do for it."

Cledra had said that the poison had been administered in Jessop's water and from what the Earl had just heard it was something that he was prepared to believe.

He therefore talked to his Head Groom and his Trainer and told them that in future the buckets containing the horses' water were not to be left outside the stalls at any time.

What was more the stables were to be strictly watched at night so that it would be impossible for anybody to enter them unseen.

Both men were surprised by the Earl's orders, but knew that they must be strictly obeyed or there would be trouble.

Because he thought that they looked at him somewhat speculatively, the Earl explained,

"I have reason to believe that there is somebody in Newmarket who might be mad enough to wish to damage my horses in some way or other and I therefore insist that you take no chances."

"I'll see to it, my Lord," his Head Groom nodded.

As he left the stable, the Earl's Trainer followed him to ask,

"Would your Lordship consider giving me any information you have not yet communicated about the danger to our horses, my Lord?"

The Earl hesitated and then decided that it would be a mistake to confide in anybody.

"I have simply heard rumours about the way that Lord Ludlow's horse, Jessop, died," he replied. "Of course there are always suspicions when a winning horse dies after a race, but I think we should take every precaution to see that my own horses are in no danger."

He was aware as he spoke that because he was so successful there would always be fanatics who might hate him for his successes, just as there were anarchists who wished to overthrow Monarchs for no personal reason but because they disapproved of them in principle.

His Trainer was silent.

And then he said,

"I understand what you are saying to me, my Lord. At the same time I admit I'm rather disappointed that you didn't buy anything at Sir Walter Melford's sale yesterday. I was hoping that you would bid for Raskal and Mandrake, if nothing else."

The Earl had expected this and he replied,

"When I saw the horses close to, I was not so impressed with them as I expected to be. But don't be disappointed. There is a sale coming up at Tattersalls in two weeks' time, where I understand there will be some exceptional animals that I shall certainly wish to add to my stable."

The Trainer smiled.

"That's good news, my Lord. Very good news!"

The Earl walked away knowing that he had left him happy.

But he was still worried in case Melford should treat any of his horses as he had treated Jessop.

The Earl was aware what a grievous blow this must have been to Lord Ludlow, considering he certainly could not afford to add to his stable, which had been sadly depleted by Jessop's death.

He made a mental note to try and help him in some way, but for the moment he could not think how he could do it without making anything he suggested sound patronising or a kind of charity, which would be humiliating.

Now driving at a speed that was the envy of every vehicle they passed, the Earl had the feeling that by carrying first Star and then Cledra out of reach of Sir Walter, he was starting a war, the outcome of which for the moment he could not anticipate.

He was quite certain from what he had heard of Sir Walter Melford that he would not take such insults lying down.

He would undoubtedly try to find out by every means in his power who was responsible for what he would consider the criminal kidnapping of his niece and her horse.

The Earl thought dryly that he could legally cause a great deal of trouble as he was after all Cledra's Guardian.

Equally he would be well aware that, if he took the case to the Magistrates while the plea of cruelty might not be valid in law, the disclosure of his behaviour would undoubtedly destroy him socially.

The Earl therefore reasoned that Sir Walter would strike secretly in his desire for revenge, using poison or any other weapon that came easily to his undoubtedly twisted mind.

With Cledra lying at his feet he could not help as he drove on having a very clear remembrance of her blood-stained back.

He told himself that only a man who was mentally deranged could have behaved in such a manner towards any woman, let alone one who was little more than a child and as delicately made as Cledra.

The Earl reasoned that, had she stayed the whole night and perhaps part of the next day tied to the manger without being attended to, she might easily have died.

The idea made him so angry that there was a scowl between his eyes as he drove on and only Eddie would have been aware of exactly what he was feeling.

*

In record time the Earl turned in at his very impressive lodge gates.

The great house that had been in the Poynton family for more than two hundred years was majestic in the afternoon sunshine, standing above a large lake spanned by a stone bridge.

But the Earl did not drive towards the house. Instead he turned left down a narrow track through the trees and drove on through his Park, scattering the speckled deer as he approached them.

It was over half-a-mile before, out of sight of the big mansion, there were gates leading into a beautiful garden filled with flowers where stood an attractive house, Queen Anne in origin, built of red brick and mellowed with age.

The Earl drew up with a flourish outside the front door and Yates jumped down to raise the brass knocker with a noisy rat-tat.

Before finally the door was opened which took a minute or two, an elderly groom had come from the stables that were hidden among the trees.

He came up to the phaeton touching his forelock respectfully.

"'Afternoon, your Lordship. Nice to see you."

"I am not stopping, Cobbler," the Earl replied, "but go to the horses' heads while Yates and I carry something inside that we have brought for her Ladyship."

"Aye, my Lord."

The Earl fixed the reins on the driving board and then as the front door opened he and Yates lifted Cledra very carefully from the floor of the phaeton and carried her into the hall.

The white-haired butler, who was rather deaf, greeted the Earl who said,

"Tell your wife, Dorkins, that I want to speak to her in the Blue Bedroom."

"My – wife, my Lord?"

"Yes, Dorkins, your wife!" the Earl repeated raising his voice.

The butler shuffled away while Yates and the Earl carried the basket with Cledra in it up the carved wooden staircase to the first floor.

There were rooms opening off each side of a large corridor, but the Earl and Yates walked on.

The Blue Bedroom was situated at the far end with windows overlooking the garden at the back and the Park at the side.

It was a pretty room and the Earl felt that any woman would appreciate the azure blue of the hangings and the white panelling that had decorated the walls since the house was first built.

They put down Cledra in her basket near the bed and now they had reached the end of their journey the Earl bent down and removed the muslin that covered her face.

She had not moved since they had left Newmarket and, because she was so still, he was wondering if the journey had been too much for her when Mrs. Dorkins came into the room.

She was an elderly woman, but she had before she married late in life, been lady's maid to the Earl's mother and he had in consequence known her ever since he had been a boy.

"Master Lennox!" Mrs. Dorkins exclaimed and then corrected herself, hastily dropping a curtsey and saying,

"I means – your Lordship."

"I want your help, Hannah."

"My help, my Lord?"

Her eyes were drawn instinctively to the basket on the ground and she walked towards it exclaiming,

"Now what can your Lordship have here?"

"Somebody who needs you to nurse her and bring her back to health," the Earl replied.

He saw the surprise in Hannah's face and added,

"I will leave Yates to explain to you what must be done and the secrecy that is necessary while I go and see my grandmother."

"Her Ladyship'll be ever so excited to see you, my Lord," Mrs. Dorkins replied. "She was only sayin' this morning that 'twas far too long since you'd paid us a visit."

"I am aware of that, Hannah, but I know that what I have to tell her Ladyship will be better medicine than any physician can supply."

He walked from the room as he spoke leaving the door open and heard as he went Yates begin a voluble explanation as to why they were here.

The Earl walked down the passage to a room in the centre of the house where his grandmother had changed what had once been a large and impressive salon into her bedroom.

As she was confined to one room and was only occasionally able to leave her bed for a chair in the window, she had insisted that her surroundings should be as attractive as possible.

She wanted the people who visited her to go away with the impression that she was not only surrounded by beauty but she herself was still beautiful as she had been when she had been acclaimed as one of the loveliest ladies that Society had ever seen.

Now the Dowager Countess was in her late seventies, but her classical features were unchanged and, although there were lines under her eyes and wrinkles, which she deplored, any artist would have found her still extremely beautiful.

In fact the Countess's success as a leader of Society had not depended entirely on her looks.

She was also intelligent and witty and made every man she met wish to see her again and not only pay her compliments but talk to her because she inspired and stimulated them.

The Earl knocked on the door and, when it was opened by a lady's maid who was also getting on in years, the woman gave what was almost a shriek of delight before she cried,

"It's *you*, my Lord! Her Ladyship's been longin' to see you and wonderin' why you've not called on her for so long."

"Well, I am here now," the Earl replied, "and it is good to see you looking so well, Emma."

The old maid curtseyed, and then left the room leaving the Earl alone with his grandmother.

A quick glance showed him that she was not in bed, but sitting in a chair by the window with an ermine rug going slightly yellow with age over her knees.

She was decked as usual in a profusion of jewels that glittered in the sunshine streaming in through the window.

The Countess never allowed anybody to see her until her hair was dressed, her face rouged and powdered as it had been when she was young and some of her fabulous and extremely valuable jewels draped round her neck and glittering on her fingers and wrists.

Now, as the Earl went towards her, she held out both her hands and the movement made her gems scintillate, so that she seemed to be enveloped in all the colours of the rainbow.

"Lennox! Where have you been, you naughty boy!" she scolded him. "I thought you had forgotten me."

The Earl kissed both his grandmother's hands and then her cheek before he sat down in the chair next to her.

"You are looking very beautiful, Grandmama," he began. "Are you waiting for some ardent beau to call upon you?"

"Flattery will get you nowhere!" the Countess replied.

At the same time she was smiling at the compliment.

"I am dressed up," she went on, "because if there is nobody else to admire me, I might as well admire myself. At this time of the year everybody is enjoying the London Season, except for me."

"I have been to Newmarket."

"I guessed that. How many races did you win?"

The Earl laughed.

"That is indeed flattery, Grandmama. Most people would have asked *if* I had won a race."

"Don't try any false modesty with me," the Countess said almost sharply. "You know as well as I do that you win and go on winning. It becomes almost boring to read *The Racing News*."

She glanced as she spoke towards the newspapers that were lying on a stool by her side and the Earl was not surprised to see among them sporting newspapers that were usually read only by gentlemen and that he never saw them in any other lady's sitting room except his grandmother's.

"As you have undoubtedly read which races I won yesterday," he replied, "I need only tell you that I was first in the Sefton Stakes with the only horse I entered today."

"Good," the Countess smiled, "then, as you are here already, you must have left Newmarket without watching the last three races."

"I left for a special reason," the Earl answered.

The way he spoke and the fact that he lowered his voice slightly made the Countess look at him quickly.

At that moment the door opened and the butler came into the room followed by a footman carrying a tray on which stood an ice cooler containing an open bottle of champagne, two glasses and a plate of very thin *pâté* sandwiches.

Both the Earl and the Countess were silent as he placed the tray on the low table and would have poured out the champagne, but the Earl said,

"I will do it, Dorkins,"

"Very good, my Lord."

The servants left the room and the Earl half-filled both glasses and handed one to his grandmother.

"You know that I am not supposed to drink alcohol," the Countess remarked.

"You will need it when you hear what I have to tell you," the Earl responded.

"I thought the moment you came into the room that you had something exciting to impart," the Countess said. "At least I hope it is exciting. I cannot tell you, Lennox, how bored I am sitting here with nobody to talk to but the servants and thinking of all the things I am now too old to enjoy."

"You will enjoy what I have to tell you and especially when I begin by saying that I have brought with me a young woman, whose presence must be a complete secret from everybody except those in your household like Hannah whom we can trust implicitly."

The Countess stared at him for a moment incredulously.

Then she said,

"A young woman? Are you telling me that you have finished with that red-haired Hungarian?"

The Earl threw back his head and laughed.

"That is so like, you, Grandmama! You tell me that you are bored here with nobody to talk to, while in fact there is nothing that happens in London that you don't know about! There has never been anybody as well informed as you."

"It is no thanks to what I learn from my grandson," the Countess replied tartly. "Now tell me the whole story. Who is this woman and why have you brought her to me?"

"Because I have kidnapped her and, quite frankly, I am rather nervous as to the consequences."

His eyes twinkled as he spoke, but, if he had meant to startle and intrigue his grandmother, he had certainly succeeded.

The Countess's eyes searched his face as if for the moment she thought that he was playing a joke on her.

Then she said with an eagerness that made her seem immeasurably younger than her years,

"Tell me what you have done and don't leave out a single detail."

*

Twenty minutes later the Earl accompanied by Yates left the Dower House and drove back the way they had come. When they reached the main drive they went towards the house as if they had just arrived from Newmarket.

There was no reason why the Earl should not call first on his grandmother. At the same time he was hoping that nobody had seen the phaeton moving beneath the thick foliage in the Park and that it would not enter anybody's head that he and Yates had rid themselves of a large basket.

When they reached the Big House, the Major Domo who supervised the whole household expressed surprise that the Earl had arrived so early.

"I must apologise, my Lord, that I was not waiting on the steps for your Lordship's return," he said. "But I was expecting you an hour or so later, thinking that your Lordship'd stay for at least the fourth race before leaving Newmarket."

"There were no horses of any particular interest in those races," the Earl replied loftily, "and I was resting on my laurels after Swallow had romped home in the Sefton Stakes."

"That's good news. Very good news, my Lord." the Major Domo beamed.

The Earl was quite certain that all his staff, not only at Poynton Hall but on all his other estates, had backed Swallow, just as they would have backed his two other horses, which had won races on the previous day.

He went into his study and sent for his Agent to give him a report on what was happening on the estate and informed the butler who was making enquiries on behalf of the chef that he would be alone for dinner.

"I want a light meal," he said. "I always find at Race Meetings one eats and drinks too much."

"That's what your Lordship's late father always used to say, my Lord," the butler replied, "and he was as abstemious as your Lordship, which was why he kept his figure to his dying day."

"I hope I shall do the same," the Earl commented.

When he was alone, the Earl took a cursory look at the newspapers before he went upstairs to bathe and change for dinner.

He had not talked to Yates when they were driving back to the house, but now as he put on his evening clothes, in which he looked even more magnificent than he did in the daytime, he said to his valet,

"Did you explain to Mrs. Dobson exactly what was necessary?"

"Yes, my Lord, and she's very skilled with wounds. She were rememberin' how she nursed you, my Lord, when you had a fall out huntin' and another time when you fell out of a tree into a gooseberry bush and scratched yourself all over."

The Earl smiled.

"I will never forget how those thorns stung and irritated me! But I was tough even as a small boy, while Miss Melford looks very delicate."

"I hope she's stronger than she looks, my Lord, and I've got some special healin' cream, which I promised to give to Mrs. Dobson. I'm wonderin' if your Lordship will be callin' at the Dower House tonight or tomorrow mornin'?"

"I think it would be wiser if I went tomorrow morning before I return to London. It is very important, Yates, that nobody should connect me or you with her Ladyship's visitor."

"I knows that, my Lord."

"In fact I hope you have impressed upon Mrs. Dobson that no one outside the household should know that she is there. It is absolutely essential that everybody else should remain in complete ignorance that she even exists."

"It's goin' to be difficult, my Lord. Servants chatter in the country worse than they does in London or even at Newmarket."

"I am aware of that," the Earl said shortly, "but gossip can indeed be dangerous, as we both know."

"Yes, my Lord," Yates agreed.

It would be some time, the Earl thought, before Sir Walter's enquiries led him to believe that Cledra's disappearance had anything to do with him.

And yet one never knew. There were so many possibilities that might end in their secret being exposed before they were ready for it.

The Earl puzzled over the whole situation, facing it as he had faced every campaign in which he had been engaged during the war in India or the revolutionaries in France, who, having seized power, were as merciless and brutal as Sir Walter Melford.

He fell asleep thinking of all the possible eventualities and how he could combat them if they did occur. And he awoke to go on planning, using his brain in a way that he had not been obliged to do for quite some time.

As he ate very little breakfast and preferred to ride alone, there was no one to notice, when having galloped off in a different direction on leaving the Big House, he rode round through empty fields and an isolated part of the Park to bring him to the Dower House.

There was no groom waiting for him at the door and he put the horse he was riding in the stable and entered the house by a side door.

He walked upstairs, but made no attempt to go to his grandmother's room, knowing that she would certainly not wish to receive him so early in the morning before she had applied her cosmetics or taken her jewels from their leather boxes, which had grown slightly worn with age.

Instead he walked along the corridor to the Blue Bedroom, knocked perfunctorily on the door and opened it before Hannah could reach it.

She dropped him a curtsey and then said as eagerly as his grandmother had spoken,

"It's good to see you, my Lord! I was hopin' you'd call on us. The young lady's awake and, as your Lordship'll understand, a little bewildered by what's happened to her."

The Earl did not answer, but walked towards the bed.

The early sunshine coming in through the window made the room glow with a golden haze.

In the light of it he saw two very large eyes staring at him and found that Cledra's small pointed face was crowned with hair that, he realised, was the colour of the first rays of the sun.

Hannah withdrew and the Earl put out his hand.

"Good morning, Cledra. How are you feeling?"

"Are you – are you – really here? And is it – possible – as that nice person has just – told me that I have been asleep for – three days?"

The Earl took her hand in his and sat down beside the bed.

"Do you remember what happened before that?" he asked quietly.

"Uncle – Walter – ! H-he does not – know I am – here?"

"He has no idea of it."

"And – Star – is s-safe?"

"Star is quite safe," the Earl replied. "But you will remember that you asked me to change his name? There is now no such horse as 'Star' but there is a new animal in my stable that has been registered as 'Winged Victory'. Also I think you will have a little difficulty in recognising him when you see him."

Cledra looked at him questioningly and he explained,

"I thought it was wise before I removed 'Winged Victory' from Newmarket to dye a certain patch on his nose so that he is now jet-black."

Cledra gave a little cry and he felt her fingers tighten on his.

"That was – clever – very clever of you. But now do you – think he is – safe?"

"I am sure he is, but we have to make very certain that you are safe too."

The expression in her eyes changed almost like a cloud passing across the sun.

"Uncle Walter was – very – very angry."

"Are you strong enough to tell me what happened?" the Earl asked.

Cledra drew in her breath.

"When I – came down very early to breakfast because it was the day of the – s-sale somebody had just told him that – Star was missing. He guessed at once that I was – responsible – and he dragged me to the stables and taking me into – Star's stall – asked me where he was."

"Did you tell him?" the Earl enquired.

"You know that was – something I would – never have done. Not only to – save Star but also to – safeguard you after – you had been so – k-kind."

"What did your uncle do then?"

"He – knocked me down because I refused to answer and then – he asked me again and I still – refused."

Cledra's voice broke and after a moment with an effort she continued in a whisper,

"When he realised that I would not tell him he – gagged me – and then he beat me until –I cannot remember – anything else."

The Earl thought that this was a good thing.

At the same time as he listened to Cledra's story without being aware of it, his fingers had tightened on hers.

Only when she gave a little exclamation of pain did he see that he had squeezed her hand until it was almost bloodless.

"Forgive me," he said. "It is just that I find it impossible to believe that any man could treat a woman in such an appalling fashion."

"H-how did you – find me?"

The Earl told her that, when he had seen a stall locked and covered with horse blankets and noticed

Star's name on it, he had thought he heard a slight whimper.

"I felt I had to go back and investigate," he told her simply.

"So you – brought me – away?"

"I took you away without, I think, anybody being aware of it," the Earl answered, "but you must take no chances. First you must get well and then we can decide where you can go where your uncle will never find you again."

Her eyes widened for a moment as she asked apprehensively,

"Y-you don't – think he will – find me here?"

"There is always a risk. That is why you will be seen only by my grandmother's elderly servants who have been with her for many years and have known me ever since I was your age and younger."

"You are – very kind, so very – very kind," Cledra cried, "but I would not – wish you to get into any trouble on – my behalf."

"I can look after myself," the Earl asserted. "It is how I can best look after you that is the difficulty."

"And – Winged Victory."

"And, of course, Winged Victory."

"I shall – want to see him when – I am better."

"As soon as you are well enough, I promise that I will ride him over here," the Earl replied, "and you can ask him if he is comfortable."

She gave a tiny chuckle that he thought was entrancing, like the sound a child would make on receiving a present.

"When he comes – I will make him thank you – as I want to do too."

"I shall look forward to that," the Earl smiled, "but now you must concentrate on getting well as quickly as possible. I am returning to London, but I shall be back very soon to see you again."

"Will you – promise to do so? Everybody here is – very kind – but you are – different."

The Earl raised his eyebrows.

"Different in what way?"

"Because you have been – so kind to Star and to me, you are our – friend."

"It is something I am delighted to be," he answered, "but you must both obey my orders and our friendship must remain a secret."

"A – secret," Cledra murmured, "and very – precious because – you are so kind."

The Earl rose to stand for a moment holding her hands and looking down at her.

"Take care of yourself," he urged, "and get well quickly. Your life will be very different in the future from what it has been with your uncle."

He felt her fingers quiver in his and then, because he felt that he must reassure her and give her confidence, he kissed her hand.

Her skin was very soft, he thought, like a child's.

Then he smiled at her and without saying anything more went from the room.

CHAPTER FOUR

The Earl was waiting in his very impressive library when the butler announced,

"Major Edward Lowther, my Lord."

The Earl rose from his desk saying,

"I am glad to see you, Eddie."

His friend did not reply, but was staring at him, not at his face but at his cravat.

"You are wearing a new style and one I have never seen before."

The Earl laughed.

"I did not expect you to be so observant. It's a variation on the one that Brummel was so cock-a-hoop about last week."

"It is better than his," Eddie replied, "which will undoubtedly infuriate him."

"Actually it is easier to tie and, as you are well aware, I dislike looking like everybody else."

"That is something you could never do," Eddie pointed out mockingly.

He took the glass of champagne that the Earl handed him and said,

"As we are alone, I hope you are going to regale me with the story that I am sure is behind your precipitate departure from Newmarket yesterday."

"I doubt if you would be interested," the Earl countered in a deliberately bored voice. "I cannot believe I was missed."

"One person remarked on your absence."

The Earl took a sip of his champagne before he asked,

"Who was that?"

"Melford!"

The Earl was still and there was a perceptible pause before he enquired,

"Do you mean, that he noticed I left early?"

"I saw him in White's this evening before I went home to dress for dinner."

"In White's?" the Earl exclaimed.

"He was the guest of that young fool, Deveraux."

"Deveraux is so dimwitted he has no idea if it is Christmas or Easter," the Earl said scornfully, "but you would think he had enough sense not to take a man like Melford into White's."

"It was quite obvious to me that he was making the most of having met a large number of those present at his sale. You might almost say that he was fawning on them."

"And you say that he mentioned me, Eddie?"

"He came up to me while I was talking to Charles Hubbart."

The Earl waited and there was a tenseness in his attitude that told Eddie that he was particularly interested in what he had to relate.

"He said, 'good evening, Lowther. I noticed that your host, Poynton, did not stay for the last three races yesterday. I wondered why he was in such a hurry to leave and where he was going'."

There was a frown between the Earl's eyes as he asked,

"Did you tell him?"

"I was just about to," Eddie replied, "when I thought that it was none of his damned business and so I replied evasively, 'my father, Sir Walter, always said that, if there was one thing more interesting than horses, it was women'."

He knew as he spoke that the Earl relaxed before he quizzed him,

"What did Melford say to that?"

"He did not say anything, but that idiot, Deveraux, laughed like a clucking hen and exclaimed, 'I know who you are talking about and in my opinion Poynton's taste is superb. Ileni Carrington is undoubtedly the most beautiful woman in London'."

The frown intensified on the Earl's forehead and, because he knew that he was angry, Eddie said hastily,

"I expected that the conversation would annoy you, but I had the feeling, although I may be wrong, that you would not wish Melford to know that you went to Hertfordshire."

The Earl thought that this was perceptive of Eddie, but he had no intention of saying how important it was that Sir. Walter should not be aware that it had been his destination.

"You were quite right not to tell him anything about me," he said, "and anyway I cannot imagine why he should be curious."

Eddie looked at him sharply and, as he walked across the room to refill his glass of champagne, he said,

"We have been in some tight corners together, Lennox, and I also helped you in some of your exploits in France. However skillful you may be there is one thing you never disguise really effectively."

"And what is that?" the Earl asked his friend truculently.

"Your eyes," Eddie replied. "The look in them now is only there when you are sensing danger, adventure or love!"

The Earl laughed.

"I had no idea that you were so observant."

"Remember when you are playing cloak-and-dagger games with anybody else to drop your eyelids and look supercilious and definitely bored, which recently has become your habitual attitude."

The Earl chuckled again.

Then he said,

"Is this true? Do I really appear bored and supercilious?"

"Add to it 'cynical' and you have the whole picture!" Eddie teased him.

"*Dammit all*, you are pulling my leg and I find it an impertinence on your part."

"It is also true," Eddie persisted, "that at this moment there is a new look in your eyes and a sudden alertness that has not been there for quite some time. I am therefore convinced that you are enjoying a chase or an adventure and I think it is extremely mean of you to count me out."

The Earl was saved having to reply because dinner was announced.

It was only when they went back to the study and were sitting in two comfortable armchairs with a decanter of brandy beside them, having talked of a great many other subjects during dinner, that Eddie returned to the attack.

"I want to know, as it is unlikely that anybody here is eavesdropping at your door," he said mockingly, "are you or are you not going to confide in me, Lennox?"

To his surprise the Earl rose to his feet to walk to the window which opened onto the garden.

There was only one house in Berkeley Square which had a private garden all its own. The other residents used the one in the centre of the Square to which they each had a key.

The Earl's garden backed on to the high wall that surrounded the garden of Devonshire House and, although it was not large, there were trees and shrubs and a profusion of flowers, the fragrance of which scented the air sweetly.

The Earl, however, was not thinking of his garden, he was thinking of Cledra and wondering if, after what Sir Walter had said to Eddie, he had an inkling as to where his niece and her horse had been taken.

Then, as if he made up his mind, he turned back to sit down once again facing his friend.

"I may be wrong," he began slowly, "to tell you what is not my secret, but I have a feeling that you might be helpful, as you have been so often in the past."

"Thank you, I am glad I have my uses!" Eddie replied sarcastically.

The Earl did not smile, instead he said,

"This is very serious, so serious that I am deeply concerned about the life of a girl and a horse."

Eddie looked at him incredulously, but he did not speak and the Earl went on,

"That is the truth for my intuition tells me that there is every chance of their both being killed!"

Eddie sat forward in his chair.

"Tell me everything from the very beginning," he suggested eagerly in much the same way as the Earl's grandmother had spoken.

"That is what I intend to do," the Earl replied, "but make no mistake, Eddie, if you are involved you may be risking your life as well!"

*

The Earl spent the next two days with the Prince Regent.

He was aware that the Prince not only extended to him his friendship but also admired him.

Because he was genuinely fond of the Heir to the Throne, the Earl did his best to prevent him from drinking too much or being imposed upon by hangers-on. They and numerous charlatans were always intent on creeping into the Royal favour by any means, however shady.

He went with the Prince Regent to watch a prize fight and he helped him to decide whether or not to buy two pictures that his advisers had told him were not worth the money he was asked for them.

The Earl, however, took the opposite view.

He thought actually the pictures were cheap and, while they were by Dutch artists and therefore not fashionable, he agreed with the Prince Regent that they were outstanding works of art and it would be a pity to miss the opportunity of adding them to his collection.

There were the usual parties in the evening, which the Earl was beginning to find monotonous because there was too much to eat and too much to drink and too often the same guests as had been entertained the previous night.

He was also not particularly elated to find himself sitting beside Ileni Carrington.

She was looking alluringly lovely with the candlelight glinting on her red hair and turning it to fire and he was aware that she was looking at him reproachfully because he had not called on her since his return to London.

Because he had not yet had time to buy her a present, as he intended to do, or write what was to all intents and purposes was a farewell letter, he could understand her perplexity regarding his remissness.

He also knew that the Prince Regent had put her next to him thinking that he was being tactful and being aware that they had been very interested in each other for the last three months.

The Earl found himself wondering now, as he had often done before, why suddenly a woman as beautiful as Ileni should pall on him for no particular reason and why, having once thought her extraordinary, he now found her very ordinary.

He appraised her in the same way that he would a picture or a jewel, deciding whether it was real or false.

While it was impossible for him not to admire her beauty and recognise that she had a grace and a presence that many other women lacked, something was missing.

He knew if he was honest that the magnetism that they had had for each other had suddenly ceased to vibrate.

His feelings for Ileni therefore had become exactly the same as he felt for any other woman at the table, most of whom were deeply intrigued by the Prince Regent or the man next to whom they were sitting.

'What is the matter with me,' the Earl asked himself, 'that I find it impossible to be faithful to any woman for more than a very short time?'

He had thought when he had first been attracted by Ileni that she was different from any other beauty he had met before, but now the fire in her eyes an her obvious desire for him was something that he was all too familiar with.

He had been intrigued by her slight accent, by the way she could make the most ordinary remark sound fascinating and by a look in her eyes that promised unknown delights that he had never sampled.

Now suddenly, like the fall of a curtain at the end of a play, his interest in her had ceased and he knew that everything she said sounded banal.

While her skin was very white in contrast with the red of her hair or her crimson provocative lips, he had no wish to touch her.

'What am I looking for? What do I want!'

He knew that it was a question he had asked before and had never found the answer.

There had been so many women in his life, all of them beautiful and all of them when he first met them exceptional, like a picture painted by a great Master, a piece of *Sèvres* china or a Greek statue.

Then inevitably, sometimes after months, sometimes after only weeks, he began to find flaws in what had first seemed perfection.

Now with Ileni the magnetism had ceased to flow from his body, or was it his mind, to hers and he knew that as far as he was concerned the curtain had fallen once again.

'One thing is quite certain,' the Earl told himself looking with unseeing eyes across the dining room table, 'I shall never marry.'

Then he knew that sooner or later he must have an heir.

The title had passed from father to son for six generations and it would be a crime for him to break the chain and allow the Earldom to go to a dull cousin who lived in Scotland, who was only interested in shooting grouse and catching salmon.

The Earl was very conscious of his duties in the House of Lords and of the part he played in the County of Hertfordshire, being well aware that, when the present Lord Lieutenant died or retired, he would step into his shoes as the representative of the King in the County.

'I shall *have* to marry one day,' he told himself despairingly.

He thought of the long years of boredom when, even if he married for love, his feelings would inevitably change and he would still be left with a wife whose conversation was repetitive of everything she had said the day before.

He knew that Eddie was right when he said that he needed adventure in his life, but was aware that what had seemed like an exploration in love always ended in a banality from which his only wish was to escape as quickly as possible.

He had exactly the same trouble where it concerned his mistresses.

He invariably chose one who had made her mark as a dancer, a singer or an actress simply because they had a glamour about them that was the reward of success.

He felt they glowed like a light until, after he had installed them in an expensive house, provided them with a carriage, horses and jewels which made them glitter like a Christmas tree, the inevitable occurred.

He would walk out of the house late one night knowing that he had no wish to see the same pretty face again, feel the same clinging arms around his neck or the same voice trying to entice another expensive present from him.

'It's finished,' he would tell himself as he drove home.

The next morning his secretary would receive the orders he had received many times before to pay off the lady in question and close the house until it should be wanted again.

'The trouble with me,' the Earl thought to himself, 'is that I think quicker and feel faster than other men. That means anything that I am interested in comes to an end quicker and that can be disastrous.'

"You are very pensive," a voice said beside him, "and I am waiting for you to tell me when I shall see you again."

The Earl did not reply and Ileni Carrington said carried on softly,

"I shall be alone tomorrow afternoon at three o'clock. Richard will be at the House of Commons."

The Earl was about to reply that he was otherwise engaged and then thought that it would be a mistake to say anything.

Tomorrow he would go to the best jewellers in Bond Street and choose her a farewell present, which he would send to her with a letter.

Accordingly he smiled and she took it to mean that he had accepted her invitation.

Then in a louder voice that could be overheard she started to amuse him with the latest gossip which he might have missed while he had been at Newmarket.

Only when the Earl said 'goodnight' did her fingers cling to his and he knew from the way she gave his hand a tiny squeeze that it was a signal that she was expecting him tomorrow.

And she had not the slightest idea that his feelings towards her had changed.

The Earl, however, was feeling irritated with himself when he and Eddie drove in his carriage back to Berkeley Square.

"Are you going home," Eddie asked, "or would you like to drop in at *The White House*? There is a very attractive new batch of ladybirds from France who are quite sensational! Or perhaps we only think so because the French have been notably absent from the houses of pleasure until the Armistice."

"I am going home," the Earl asserted firmly.

"Still worrying about Melford?" Eddie asked. "I think you are making him out to be more of a 'bogey' than is necessary."

He thought that the Earl stiffened and added quickly,

"I am appalled at the way he treated his niece and if you are right he ought to be shot for poisoning Ludlow's horse. But I cannot believe he will continue to add crime upon crime, knowing that if he does he will be certain, sooner or later, to hang for it."

"Madmen are not reasonable," the Earl pointed out.

"You think he is mad?"

"I am sure of it!"

"Then, of course, he is a danger," Eddie agreed, "and we ought to rid ourselves of him before he runs amok like a dog with rabies."

"That is easier said than done," the Earl replied. "I have no wish to hang for Melford or for anybody else for that matter."

"You were not so particular in France and, when you brought the D'Orcys out of prison by what I may say was a miracle, you left quite a lot of bodies behind you or so they told me at the time."

"I was younger in those days. I have grown more careful with age and have begun to think not only of my reputation but also of my life."

Eddie laughed.

"Equally I thought that tonight you were not enjoying yourself and, if you are to persist in fighting a crusade to save this girl and her horse, you may as well enjoy it."

"I am enjoying it, as it happens," the Earl answered, "but the last thing I want is for anybody to suspect that I am involved with Melford, whom I loathe and detest."

It suddenly struck Eddie that the Earl's boredom during the dinner party had not been because he was worried over his 'crusade' as he called it, but because he was not enjoying himself with Ileni Carrington.

He had suspected before the Earl went to Newmarket that he was not as interested in her as he had been previously.

Yet when she had been so obviously delighted to see him this evening, he told himself that he had been mistaken and they were just as close as they had ever been.

Now he recalled that when once or twice he had glanced at the Earl during dinner he had seemed preoccupied and was not as engrossed with Ileni as he would have expected.

He wanted to ask his friend frankly if the *affaire de coeur* was at an end.

But he knew, close though he was to the Earl and, although they had been together in many tight corners and had shared both dangerous and joyous occasions, there was one thing he dared not probe into and that was the Earl's private life when it came to love.

The horses drew up in Berkeley Square and the Earl enquired,

"Are you coming in for a drink or do you wish my carriage to carry you home?"

"I will come in for a drink," Eddie said, "but send the horses away, I will walk back."

The Earl knew that Eddie's house, which belonged to his father, was no further away than Curzon Street. He therefore dismissed the carriage and they both went into the house.

In the library there was champagne and other drinks waiting for them, but the Prince Regent's hospitality had been over-generous and neither Eddie nor the Earl wanted anything more to drink.

Then, as if he read his mind, the Earl said,

"Tomorrow, as it is Friday, I intend to go home. Are you coming with me?"

"Of course, if you want me to."

"I always want you," the Earl replied, "and I think, as you know the secret I am hiding, it would be a good idea if you met Cledra and helped me think what I can do with her once she is well enough to travel."

"You are sending her away?"

"If she was younger I would have sent her to school," the Earl answered, "but I can hardly leave her indefinitely with my grandmother in case Melford discovers where she is hiding."

He was speaking almost as if he were talking to himself.

"There are only old servants in the Dower House who would not know what to do if he tried to snatch her away or ill-treat her."

"You can hardly take her to The Hall," Eddie remarked.

"I am aware of that, but I have been wondering if I should find a chaperone of some sort and send her to the house I have in Cornwall. You have been there once, do you remember?"

"Of course I remember it," Eddie replied. "It's a lovely place, but she might be frightened there by herself and very bored with no one to talk to."

"I have a feeling that she might be quite happy as long as she had her horse with her," the Earl said. "At the same time it could be dull for her, or worse still, she would be very vulnerable if her uncle found out where she was."

Eddie was about to tease the Earl for being so concerned about a young girl, who he had said was little more than a child and with whom he had such a short acquaintance.

Then he knew that the Earl was almost fanatical in the way that he loathed cruelty.

If his story was true, which Eddie knew it was, then the punishment that Melford had inflicted on his niece was something that the Earl would be determined to revenge, however long it took him.

Aloud he said,

"Because I am quite convinced, Lennox, that you are determined to get even with Melford sooner or later and teach him a lesson he will never forget, the best thing would be to get it over quickly. Why not pick some excuse for a duel with him? You are a superb shot and he would not have a chance."

"That is exactly why it is something I could not do," the Earl replied.

"That wretched child did not have much chance when he was beating her," Eddie commented dryly.

"It could also," the Earl replied as if he was again following the train of his own thoughts, "hurt Cledra if it became known how her uncle had treated her or if she was involved in any way."

Eddie realised that this was true.

If the Earl did fight a duel with Sir Walter, it would be the talk of London and the reason for it would be a question that everybody would ask.

"You are right, Lennox!" he exclaimed. "That was a stupid suggestion, but how else can we annihilate him short of pushing him into the Thames and holding his head under?"

"We will find an opportunity sooner or later," the Earl answered, "and I can only hope that he will not do too much damage in the meantime."

Eddie knew that once again the Earl was thinking of Cledra and it surprised him.

Half an hour later he announced,

"Goodnight Lennox. I must go home."

Stepping into Berkeley Square and turning left towards Curzon Street, Eddie walked slowly because he had a great deal to think about.

Whatever he had expected to hear from the Earl, it had certainly not been the story that he had regaled him with the night before last and he thought now that the whole problem was larger than he had imagined at first.

It was certainly occupying the Earl's mind to the exclusion of all else.

'It will do him good,' he decided. 'He has been more bored lately than I have ever known him. Now he seems to have woken up and is back to his old self and when he is like this he is the most exciting man I have ever met.'

He was also anticipating how much he would enjoy himself as he always did at Poynton Hall.

When he reached home, he went on thinking about the Earl until he fell asleep.

*

The Earl had said that as he had something to do in the morning that involved, although he did not tell

Eddie so, buying a present for Ileni. They would leave at about eleven-thirty, which would get them comfortably to The Hall in time for luncheon.

He ordered his phaeton and chose to drive a new team of bays that were not quite as spectacular as his chestnuts.

But they were a recent purchase and he was interested to see how they were shaping up.

He also told the two outriders who were accompanying him to ride horses that were in his London stable but which he had not yet taken to the country.

He had decided that one would make an excellent jumper and he intended to try him over the Steeplechase Course that he had just erected at The Hall.

He was as usual looking forward to going home for, whatever other houses he owned, The Hall was to him his real home and of far more consequence than any of his other possessions.

He told his secretary to send invitations to various local people, whom he found amusing, to dine with him on Saturday night and thought that Eddie would enjoy their company as much as he did.

When he came back from Bond Street with a very expensive but exquisitely designed piece of jewellery for Ileni, he wrote her a note which he knew would make it clear what the present meant.

It was now waiting to be delivered to Ileni at her house in Park Street at three o'clock when, as she had told the Earl, her husband would be in the House of Commons.

"Is everything ready?" he asked the butler after handing him the package.

"The phaeton should be round in five minutes, my Lord."

"That will just give me time to change."

The Earl went upstairs to find Yates waiting for him with a more comfortable driving coat than the one he had worn in Bond Street.

"Are you changing your Hessians, my Lord?" Yates enquired.

The Earl hesitated as to whether he should put on a pair of the new boots with the turned- over tops that Beau Brummel had just made fashionable.

Then he shook his head.

"These new Hessians are quite comfortable. But they still need breaking in, so I will keep them on."

"Very good, my Lord."

Yates was well aware that the Earl, while meticulous about his appearance, unlike the dandies. preferred to wear clothes that were comfortable rather than spectacular.

He therefore gave the impression, while being exceedingly smart, of wearing his clothes as if they were a part of him and he was therefore completely unselfconscious about them.

"You will be following me in the brake," the Earl said, as he was ready to leave the room, "and when you reach The Hall find out, but very carefully, whether there have been any enquiries made about Miss Melford or her horse."

"I've thought of that already, my Lord," Yates replied, "and your Lordship can trust me to be ever so discreet."

"I do trust you, as you well know," the Earl answered, "but make no mistake, Yates, we are dealing here with a cunning and crafty villain."

"I knows that, my Lord, and, if you've been worryin' about the young lady, so have I. She wouldn't be able to stand up to that treatment another time."

"No, that is true," the Earl agreed, "so we must make sure that there is not another time."

"We'll do that, my Lord."

The Earl walked downstairs and, glancing at the clock, saw that it was two minutes to half-past.

Having been a soldier, Eddie was a good timekeeper and the Earl was quite certain that he would not keep him waiting.

He went to his desk in the library to pick up some papers that his secretary had left for him, but which he had not yet had time to read.

They concerned improvements that were to be made on his estate in Hertfordshire, the repairs that were required on his Hunting Lodge in Leicestershire and plans for a new almshouse that he had ordered to be built before Christmas on some land he owned in Kent.

He was just wondering which he should read first when the door of the library opened and Eddie came in.

The Earl looked up with a smile.

"On the minute," he exclaimed. "I was just going to accuse you of keeping me waiting."

Then he saw the expression on his friend's face and asked,

"What is the matter? What has happened?"

Eddie walked to the desk and, as he faced the Earl across it, he said,

"I hardly know how to tell you this. I thought it must be a coincidence, but after what you have told me I am afraid it is not."

"What are you talking about?" the Earl asked sharply.

There was a pause before Eddie spoke in a voice that hardly sounded like his own,

"Ileni Carrington was found dead this morning!"

For a moment the Earl thought that either Eddie must be joking or he had not heard him aright.

Then, as he did not speak, Eddie said,

"It is true, Lennox. I have just come from the Club and they were talking of nothing else."

"What happened?"

Eddie sat down on a chair before he replied,

"Everybody was saying how extraordinary her death was. According to her uncle, who had been sent for as her parents are not in this country, she drove back from the party and went immediately to bed."

"Was Carrington at home?"

"No. He was attending a Parliamentary dinner given for some Foreign Statesman who is visiting this country at the present time."

"Go on."

"He came back two hours after his wife and, because he was late and did not wish to disturb her, he slept in another room."

The Earl did not say anything, but he knew that Ileni and her husband had occupied separate rooms for some time.

But that was irrelevant to what had happened and he merely asked,

"There was nothing wrong with her when she went to bed?"

"Her lady's maid said that she was in good spirits and not overtired," Eddie replied.

The Earl waited and he went on,

"Carrington told the doctors that he was awoken at five o'clock this morning by his wife's screams and went into her bedroom."

"What was wrong?"

"She was in an agony of pain, throwing herself about and unable to keep still."

"What did he do?"

"He rang for her maid, then thinking that it would be sometime before the woman answered, he ran to the top of the stairs and shouted to the night footman in the hall to fetch a doctor."

"I suppose that would also have taken time," the Earl remarked reflectively.

"When Carrington went back into the bedroom, his wife was lying on the floor and she appeared to be dead, except that she was twitching all over."

The Earl immediately remembered the description of how Jessop had died.

"Twitching all over," he murmured beneath his breath.

"That is how it was described by Carrington to Ileni's uncle," Eddie said. "It apparently made a deep impression on him."

"But she was dead."

"Yes, she was dead," Eddie agreed. "By the time the doctor arrived, there was nothing he could do."

"What did they say was the cause of her death?"

"Mrs. Carrington's uncle said when he asked him that question at White's that he thought that she must have had a fit of some sort."

"There was no suspicion of poison?"

"Actually I asked him that question." Eddie replied, "and the answer was that there had been no complaints from anybody else at the dinner party."

The eyes of the two men met and the Earl sighed,

"What we are both thinking must be impossible."

"That is exactly what I thought. At the same time it is a strange coincidence. After what you told me about Ludlow's horse, I made some enquiries about poisons yesterday from a friend of mine who has spent many years of his life in the East."

The Earl was listening intently.

"He said," Eddie continued, "that both the Indians and the Chinese have poisons that leave no trace and that no autopsy, however skilfully done in this country, can diagnose whether or not a victim has died of them."

"How would Melford get hold of a poison of that sort?" the Earl asked.

"I had intended today, if you had not asked me to go to the country with you," Eddie replied, "to make enquiries as to whether he had ever been in the East or was known to associate with people who had. I do not feel that it will get us very much further, but I think that any clue concerning what is occurring could be of great importance."

"You are right there," the Earl nodded.

"What is vital," Eddie went on, as if the Earl had not spoken, "is to find out if he connects you with Cledra's disappearance or whether he is just getting his own back because you bought nothing at his sale."

"I can answer that question quite simply," the Earl replied harshly. "He must be connecting me with Cledra's disappearance and he is sure that I am hiding her horse. That is why Ileni died. Now we have to act quickly to prevent him from murdering anybody else!"

*

Both the Earl and Eddie were silent as they drove out of London and Eddie was aware that the Earl, which was unlike him, was pushing his horses to a greater speed than was usual.

It was not only difficult to speak when they were travelling so swiftly but Eddie was also aware that the Earl was turning over and over in his brain what had happened.

He was trying to find a solution to one of the most intriguing and at the same time frightening situations that he had ever been confronted with.

What they were facing was cold-blooded murder and it was only because they knew of Sir Walter Melford's previous activities that they had any grounds for thinking that he might be involved.

But there was nothing they could say in a Court of Justice or anywhere else that would not endanger Cledra and would in fact not be laughed at as having no substance in fact.

Lord Ludlow's horse Jessop had died of a 'fit'. Ileni had died of a 'fit'.

But how could there be proved to be any connection between the two?

If a Guardian saw fit to beat his niece for misbehaviour, then the Law upheld his right to do so and would consider it a proper punishment for any young person who stepped out of line.

To Eddie the whole situation seemed a hopeless maze in which there was no way out, but he knew that the Earl was never defeated whatever the odds against him.

All he could hope was that he would act quickly before another innocent person was murdered.

They reached the lodge gates at Poynton Hall in ten minutes under the Earl's previous record. Eddie felt quite breathless with the speed they had travelled and sympathised with the horses who were sweating and the outriders who had found it hard to keep up with them.

The Earl brought his team to a standstill just inside the gates and then beckoned to the outriders who came to the side of the phaeton.

"Go on to the house," he ordered, "and tell them that we shall be a little late for luncheon, but I have a message to convey to her Ladyship."

The outriders touched the peaked caps they wore over their white wigs respectfully and one of them replied,

"Very good, my Lord."

The Earl turned his horses down the narrow path which led to the Dower House and, as they reached the front door, Yates clambered down to run to the horses' heads.

Eddie followed the Earl into the hall.

"Her Ladyship will see me?" the Earl asked the old butler.

"I thinks her Ladyship guessed you might be coming, my Lord," Dorkins replied. "She asked for a bottle of champagne nigh on an hour ago."

The Earl hurried up the stairs and Eddie following thought that the Earl's intuition, which was so much a part of his character, must have been inherited.

He knocked on his grandmother's door and it was opened immediately by Emma who curtseyed respectfully as he went in.

"Good morning, Grandmama," the Earl said as he walked across the room. "I have brought Eddie Lowther with me. He is one of your most fervent admirers and I could not leave him outside."

"Why should you?" the Countess asked as the Earl kissed her. "I am always ready to welcome a handsome young man. I see too few of them these days."

She held out her hand to Eddie who kissed it and said,

"I need not tell you, ma'am, that you are looking more beautiful than ever and you never grow any older."

"Flatterer!" the Countess laughed. "But there is nothing I enjoy more."

Then she looked at the Earl and declared,

"I had a feeling in my bones, as the servants say, that you would come today."

"I was coming anyway," the Earl replied. "Then I learnt something before I left which has brought me here post haste."

The way he spoke made the Countess look at him sharply.

"What has happened?" she asked.

"Ileni Carrington died last night with exactly the same symptoms and I believe from the same poison as did Ludlow's horse."

The Countess did not exclaim at the news or even start.

She merely asked,

"What do you intend to do about it?"

"I have been thinking about that as I drove here, but, because we travelled so fast, I have not yet been able to discuss it with Eddie who by the way knows our secret."

"I guessed that he would have to be brought into it," the Countess said with a smile at Eddie.

Then she turned again to her grandson.

"I know you are worried about this, but I am sure that Cledra, who is a delightful girl, will be safe here with me."

"She will be safe with you," the Earl replied, "but not here."

The Countess stared at him.

"What are you saying?"

"I have been thinking that it is important that you should both move to The Hall. There are more servants to guard you, it would be almost impossible for anybody to enter the house unobserved and I could be with you."

He knew as he spoke that his grandmother was surprised at the suggestion.

Then, with a spirit and courage that he thought afterwards he might have expected from her, she answered,

"I always enjoyed myself when I lived at The Hall and I can see no reason why I should not do so again. Certainly, dear Lennox, I am delighted to accept your invitation, although you may have some difficulty in moving me there."

"You will be guarded properly," the Earl stated, "and I have a feeling, Grandmama, that we have to be prepared for an assault from a dangerous and very wily man, who is not only evil but also mad."

CHAPTER FIVE

It was three o'clock in the afternoon by the time the Earl had everything settled to his satisfaction and his orders had reached every department at the Hall.

He and Eddie rode back to the Dower House followed by a carriage drawn by two outstanding horses to carry the Countess and Cledra and a brake for the luggage and the servants.

The Earl had given instructions before he left that Mrs. Dorkins was to come to The Hall to look after Cledra.

He had no wish for his own servants to see the condition of her back and he knew that Hannah would not gossip or tell anybody what had happened to her.

Yates had already told him that Hannah had informed the servants at the Dower House that Cledra had suffered from an accident and the Earl thought that this was a very acceptable explanation for her illness that nobody would question.

It was a sunny day with just a touch of wind to alleviate the heat and he enjoyed the ride across the Park, which brought them almost too quickly to the Dower House.

They left their horses with a groom and, as the Earl walked into the house, the old butler said,

"Her Ladyship will be ready in a few minutes, my Lord. And the young lady has asked if your Lordship would speak to her in the drawing room."

The Earl glanced at Eddie who, realising that it would be best for Cledra to speak to him alone, said,

"I will go into the study. Call me when you are ready to leave."

The Earl nodded and walked across the hall to the large attractive drawing room, which had French windows opening into the garden.

As he entered, Cledra was standing by one of them gazing out at the flowers and he thought the sun on her hair made it seem as if she wore a halo of light.

She was deep in thought and so was not aware of him until he was halfway across the room.

Then, as if she felt his presence by instinct rather than sound, she turned and he saw the expression of joy in her huge eyes.

He realised that she was thinner than when he had first met her and the white muslin gown she was wearing, which he had guessed had been made by Hannah, made her ethereal in appearance, as if she was not human, but some celestial being who had found herself unexpectedly on Earth.

There was, however, a faint colour in her pale cheeks that made her look very different from when he had last seen her.

She did not speak and, when he reached her side, he asked,

"How are you, Cledra? I hope this move will not be too much for you."

"No, of course not, my Lord."

Then, as if addressing him formally made her remember his importance, she gave him a little curtsey.

"You wanted to see me?" the Earl asked at length.

Cledra drew in her breath and looked away from him as if she was shy.

"What is worrying you?" he asked.

"Your grandmother has – told me what has – happened," she replied, "and I think that – Star and I should go – away as soon as possible."

"Go where?"

"Anywhere. But we must not bring – you trouble or into – d-danger."

The way she spoke the last word told the Earl how conscious she was of the menace that hung over them.

"I have said that I will look after you and that is what I intend to do."

Cledra clasped her hands together and raised her eyes to his.

"If anything – happened to your grandmother," she said in a voice that trembled, "or to you – I could never forgive myself. Please – let me go away – only I am afraid you will have to give me a little m-money – as I have none."

The Earl looked at her as if to make quite certain that what she was suggesting was not just a pose or something that she felt conventionally she should say, but it was impossible not to believe the sincerity he saw in her eyes.

"Supposing I agreed to such a suggestion," he asked after a moment, "how do you think you could manage on your own?"

"It is – it is something I – have to do in the future," Cledra replied, "for I dare not go to any –

friends or the few relatives Papa and Mama have in different parts of the country for fear that Uncle – Walter might k-kill them as he – killed your – your f-friend."

It was hard to say the words and the Earl saw that her hands were trembling.

He thought that few women, certainly none who he was acquainted with, would be so unselfish or so self-sacrificing.

He was also sure that Cledra had no understanding of the dangers that she would encounter if she rode off on her own.

He knew also that, because she was so sensitive and had been through an experience that would render most women prostrate, to find herself without anybody to turn to would be terrifying.

Because, however, he thought it would be a mistake to over-dramatise the situation he said lightly,

"Even if you are ready to go away, I doubt if Winged Victory would be willing to give up the comfort of his stable and the very good food he is enjoying as my guest."

"I-I could leave him – with you and go alone."

"Again I can only ask you where you would go?" the Earl questioned.

"I was – thinking after her Ladyship told me what had – happened that perhaps I could find a small – village where I could stay."

"And what would you do?"

"I could – perhaps teach children – or I can – cook quite well."

She was so small and delicately made that the Earl found it impossible to imagine her working in any menial position or being immune, wherever she was, from the attentions of men who would find her very attractive.

Because he knew that to say so would frighten her more than she was already, although she was making an effort to hide her fears, he said in what he knew would be a different tone from what she expected,

"I find it very hurtful, Cledra, that you don't trust me."

"Oh – but I do!" she cried. "How could I not trust you when you have been so kind – so very – very kind?"

"And you said we were friends."

"Yes, I know. But when I came to you in – desperation asking you to save Star from that cruel man – I had no idea that I would bring such – trouble upon you or that Uncle Walter would do anything so – w-wicked as to kill somebody you – "

She stopped speaking and the Earl knew that she had been about to say the word '*loved*'.

He thought that it was inevitable that his grandmother in telling the story of Ileni's death had made it clear that she had played a rather special part in his life.

Even if she had not said so, he was sure that Cledra was too intelligent not to realise that Sir Walter's reason for killing Ileni was his knowledge that it would hurt him personally.

"What has happened cannot be undone," the Earl said quietly. "What you have to do now, Cledra, is to help me to protect my grandmother and my horses, including, of course, Winged Victory."

"Perhaps the only – sensible way I can do – that is to return – to – Uncle Walter!"

The Earl looked at her incredulously, feeling that she could not be sincere in suggesting such a solution, but before he could speak Cledra said in a low voice,

"Perhaps if I – apologise profusely for what I have – done he will forgive me – and not – punish me as he did before."

She could not prevent the tremor in her voice and the Earl was aware that her whole body was tense, as if she was forcing herself to accept the suggestion that she was making to him.

There was silence for a moment.

Then the Earl said softly,

"Look at me, Cledra."

Obediently she turned her face up to his and he saw the terror that lay in the depths of her eyes.

But there was no sign of tears and he was aware that she had a courage that he not only admired but felt was almost incredible.

"Do you really think," he asked harshly, "that I would allow any woman, or man for that matter, if I could prevent them from doing so, to have anything to do with your uncle at this present moment? He is not only a criminal and a murderer, he is also mad."

Cledra's eyes dropped before his.

"I thought – that when I was – with him."

"We therefore have to prevent him from committing any more crimes against innocent people," the Earl asserted, "and because you know him better than anybody else, I need your help, Cledra."

She glanced at him as if to make sure that what he was saying was true and he was not inventing an excuse to save her embarrassment.

"Suppose you trust me," he suggested, "as I have asked you to do. I shall be very disappointed if you refuse."

"You know I will do – anything you want me to," Cledra replied. "It is just – that I am so ashamed and humiliated that – you have become – involved."

"Well, I *am* involved," the Earl answered, "and perhaps, because I happen to be in a different position from most people, it is better that it should be me than somebody who would feel quite unable to cope with the whole drama."

"That is true," Cledra said quickly. "You are so – wonderful and so – magnificent that I am sure that only you could – prevent Uncle Walter from doing any more – terrible and ghastly things."

"I can at least try. And now, if you are ready, I think we should take my grandmother to The Hall and get her into bed there as quickly as possible."

"Yes – of course."

Cledra picked up her bonnet that was lying on one of the chairs and with it a long stole of pale blue satin.

She put on the bonnet and tied the ribbons under her chin, taking only a perfunctory glance at her appearance in the mirror over the mantelpiece.

Then, as she saw the Earl watching her, she explained,

"Your grandmother has been kind enough to lend me this pretty bonnet and Hannah made me this gown. I can only say how – grateful I am and I do apologise for being such, a – nuisance."

"But a very charming one," the Earl said with a smile, "and, when we reach The Hall, you will find that I have brought quite a number of gowns for you from London."

Cledra stared at him in astonishment.

"B-but how did you – do that?" she stammered.

"I could hardly leave you here with nothing to wear but my nightshirt," he replied with a grin.

He saw the colour come into her cheeks and he thought that it was a long time since he had seen a woman blush so prettily,

"I think," she said after a moment, "that you will soon grow tired of my saying 'thank you', thank you – *thank you.*"

The Earl smiled again and walked towards the door.

"Come along. New gowns are not the only things I want to show you when we reach my house."

Cledra hurried after him and, as they reached the hall, the Countess was being carried downstairs in a chair by two stalwart young footmen.

She was glittering with jewels and wore, the Earl noticed with a twinkle in his eye, a bonnet with a high brim edged with lace that was the very latest fashion.

He was quite certain that, although his grandmother had for the last year found it impossible to leave her bedroom, it had not prevented her from keeping abreast of all the latest fashions and acquiring bonnets, sunshades and pelisses just for the pleasure of owning them.

When the footmen reached the hall, they set the Countess and her chair down on the marble floor and the Earl kissed her hand.

"You look so smart, Grandmama," he said, "I feel that I should be taking you to Vauxhall where you could be properly admired."

"You have taken the words out of my mouth!" Eddie said who had come from the study without waiting for the Earl to call him.

He too kissed the Countess's hand and added,

"May I say your bonnet is the prettiest I have ever seen. It completely eclipses the one worn by Mrs. Fitzherbert last Sunday."

The Countess tossed her head.

"I was never a great admirer of that woman!"

The Earl laughed.

"If you are going to gossip, may I point out that the horses are waiting and finding it very hot in the sunshine."

"And nothing can be more important than that the horses should not be incommoded," the Countess murmured mockingly.

The two footmen lifted her chair again and carried it outside to where the carriage was waiting.

Then the Earl and Eddie lifted her very gently onto the back seat of the carriage, which was made comfortable with a large number of extra cushions. There was also a rest for her legs before they were covered with a rug.

Cledra climbed in beside her, then the coachman whipped up the horses and they started slowly down the drive.

Once they were in the Park, the Earl and Eddie rode like outriders on either side of the carriage.

Only the Earl was aware that both the coachman and the footmen on the box were armed and that he carried a pistol in the pocket of his coat.

There was, however, nothing to disturb them and the only movement in the Park was made by the flutter of pigeons in the trees as they passed underneath them and by the deer who were frightened by such a cavalcade invading a domain that was usually exclusively theirs.

It all looked very beautiful in the sunshine that turned the lake to gold.

Cledra looking at it with wide eyes gave an exclamation of delight when she saw the white and black swans swimming under the bridge and the Earl's standard flying above the house itself.

"It is all so enchanting," she said to the Countess. "It cannot be true. I feel I must be dreaming."

"That is how I felt when I came here as a bride."

"You too must have been so beautiful, ma'am – that you looked like a Fairy Princess," Cledra cried.

"That is what my husband thought," the Countess answered softly, "and I knew that I was very lucky to be married to such a handsome man who was very much in love with me.

She saw that Cledra was listening wide-eyed and went on,

"My grandson is very like him and it is not surprising that so many women break their hearts over him."

"I can understand that," Cledra said, "but Hannah says that he has never asked any of them to marry him. Perhaps one day he will find a Fairy Princess like you, ma'am."

The Countess sighed.

"That is what I hope and pray, but Lennox unfortunately grows bored very quickly and the beauties he spends his time with are already married."

Cledra gave a little start.

Hannah had told her of how many lovely women had sighed for the Earl and lost their hearts to him, but she had not mentioned that they were married!

Cledra had imagined that they were young girls, who were ambitious to become his wife,

Now she thought it very strange that the husbands of the beautiful ladies were not jealous or did not do anything to prevent their wives from falling in love with the Earl.

Then, almost as if she was exploring new territory in her mind, she heard her mother saying to her father,

"How can we have been so lucky, darling, as to have found each other and be so happy while everybody else we know is always looking round for new attractions?"

"And finding them," her father had finished mockingly.

He put his arm round his wife as he added,

"The truth is I have never seen anyone as beautiful as you are or met anybody I would rather talk to than you."

Her mother had put out her hand to touch his cheek.

"Is that true – really true?"

"You know it is, my precious," her husband had replied, "and you are quite right, darling, nobody could be luckier than we are and to be poor is a very small price to pay for it."

As she was thinking over this conversation, Cledra watched the Earl ride ahead of them over the bridge as if he was leading the way.

She was aware as he did so, how brilliantly he rode, how handsome he looked on his stallion, which, with the exception of Star, she told herself was the finest horse that she had ever seen.

'That is the sort of love he needs to find,' she thought, 'and because he is an idealist he will never be content with anyone or anything that is not perfect.'

Her thoughts were interrupted by the Countess who was saying,

"It is so exciting for me to be coming home. The Hall will always really be home to me because I was so happy here."

Because she spoke wistfully and Cledra sensed that she was thinking of her husband who was dead, she slipped her hand into hers.

"Please, let me try to make you happy again, ma'am," she said. "It is my fault that you have been put to so much inconvenience and I want to try in every way I can to make it up to you."

The Countess smiled.

"Thank you, child, and let me say that I am enjoying the inconvenience because it is an adventure and something I have not been part of for a long time."

Nevertheless by the time the Countess had been carried out of the carriage, greeted the servants who welcomed her in the hall and had been carried up the great staircase escorted by the Major Domo, the housekeeper, the Earl, Eddie and Cledra, she was beginning to grow tired.

They carried her along the corridor filled with furniture and pictures that made Cledra want to stop and admire them until, after walking for what seemed a very long way, the Earl said,

"I have not put you in your usual rooms, Grandmama, because I want you near me."

His grandmother did not miss that there was a meaning in what he said.

But she merely smiled as she was carried into a very beautiful room, which was next door to the

Master suite that she and her husband had always occupied until he had died and his son had then come into the title.

"Queen Charlotte's Bedroom!" she exclaimed. "I have always thought it a very pretty room."

"I hope you will be comfortable, Grandmama," the Earl said, "and your boudoir as you will know is next door. Cledra will be just across the passage."

He did not add that her room also was near to his, but Cledra, who was listening, was aware that this was the reason why she had been put there.

She was not surprised to learn that Eddie was next to her.

"A very sensible arrangement," she heard the Countess say and knew that she was shrewdly aware of why they were sleeping so close together in a house so large that it could accommodate a Regiment of soldiers.

Emma bustled in to say that the Countess must go to bed immediately and rest after all the excitement and shooed them out of the bedroom.

Then Cledra went into her room to find that Hannah was already there.

It was a lovely room, not quite as impressive as the one where the Countess was sleeping, but larger than any bedroom that Cledra had ever occupied and very luxuriously furnished.

Without saying anything Hannah went to the wardrobe and opened it and Cledra gave a little cry of astonishment.

There were at least half-a-dozen gowns hanging there, all of them in the very latest fashion and so pretty that she could only stare at them spellbound for a few moments.

Then she asked,

"How can his Lordship have bought all these for me and – how did he know that they would fit me?"

"I gave his Lordship your measurements," Hannah replied, "when you arrived at the Dower House."

"He must have been very quick."

"His Lordship's had plenty of practice in choosin' pretty gowns for pretty women!"

Hannah spoke proudly as if it was an achievement like winning a race or bagging the largest number of game birds.

Cledra was puzzled.

As the Earl was not married, she could not understand how he should ever be in the position of buying pretty gowns for pretty women.

Then she thought perhaps he was kind to his poorer relatives who would certainly appreciate a gown or a bonnet as a Christmas present rather than chocolates or *objets d'art*.

'However he acquired such knowledge,' she thought, 'I am certainly very grateful.'

She had thought the muslin gown that Hannah had made her was very attractive, but, when she put on one of the gowns that came from London, she knew that it gave her a better figure and was more flattering than anything she had ever worn before.

The only difficulty in changing her gown was that any movement of that sort was inclined to hurt her back.

It was still bandaged, but the scars, which had bled, were now healing although sometimes at night they were very painful or itched in a manner that made it impossible to sleep.

But she knew that every day she grew stronger.

"Now don't you go doin' too much, miss," Hannah admonished her in much the same way as her Nanny would have done. "You can go down to tea with his Lordship, then you must come back and rest afore dinner."

"Do you – suppose that his Lordship will ask me to dine – with him?" Cledra asked.

"I expect so, miss, as you're a guest here," Hannah replied.

Cledra was doubtful however, feeling that the Earl might think she was too young or else that it would be best for her to have a tray in his grandmother's room as she had done at the Dower House.

She went to see how the Countess was before she went downstairs, but Emma whispered that her Mistress was having a little nap and it would be best for her to come back later.

Cledra went downstairs feeling excited at the beauty of the house, stopping on almost every stair to look at the pictures in the Great Hall and the flags that hung on either side of the stone mantelpiece.

She guessed that these had been worn by ancestors of the Earl in the battles that they had fought in.

The butler was waiting to tell her that the Earl was having tea in the Orangery and he then led her through the house to where, attached to a side wall, was an Orangery, which had been built a hundred years ago and was architecturally one of the finest in the country.

All the windows, which could be closed in the winter, were opened on both sides of it and the building was not only filled with orange trees that had been imported specially from Spain, but there were also flowers of every description. These included many species of orchids that Cledra had never seen before.

Tea was laid out so near to one of the windows that they might have been actually sitting in the garden and the Queen Anne silver, which had been presented by the Queen herself to one of the Earl's ancestors, glittered in the sunshine.

There was every sort of sandwich and various cakes set out on a service of Crown Derby.

There was also the Earl standing gazing out over the lawns, so much a part of the magnificence of the house, Cledra thought, that he seemed to blend into it almost as if he had been there for as many years as the building itself.

He turned at her approach and watched her coming towards him through the flowers and when she reached his side he said,

"You look exactly as I hoped you would in the gowns I chose for you."

"How – could you give me – anything so marvellous – and what can – I say?" Cledra asked.

"There is no need for you to say anything."

"I cannot believe that I have such lovely gowns to wear and they are really mine! Mama and I used to make lists of what we would buy if we could ever afford it."

She drew in her breath.

"Sometimes I would draw the sort of gown I would want if Papa suddenly became a millionaire – but they were only – dreams."

"Now your dreams have come true," the Earl smiled, "and that is very satisfactory, Cledra, and exactly what I would want you to feel."

"And you could – only be in a – dream, just as this house is a Fairy Palace, which I am afraid may vanish – at midnight."

The Earl laughed.

"I sincerely hope it will not do so, especially as it has survived for so many centuries already."

He was, however, touched by the way she spoke and thought that few women would express their gratitude so prettily or indeed be so grateful.

He had given so many presents in his life, but had always been expected to give more.

He had sometimes imagined that when a woman saw him she not only lifted her lips to his before he invited them, but at the same time she had her greedy little hands in his pocket.

Now he thought that it was Cledra's youth that not only made her so grateful but made everything that was happening to her seem to be part of a Fairytale.

'Soon, because she is very lovely,' he thought, 'she will become spoilt, blasé and inevitably a bore like every other woman I have known.'

He heard footsteps coming into the Orangery and knew that it was Eddie coming to join them.

Then, as he approached, the Earl felt Cledra move closer to him and thought for one second that she was becoming possessive like other women who also resented a *tête-à-tête* with him being interrupted.

To his astonishment, as Eddie reached them, he saw that Cledra's eyes held an undoubted look of fear.

For one moment he did not understand.

Then it suddenly struck him that, because of the way she had suffered at her uncle's hands, she was now, strange though it might seem, frightened of men!

For the moment he thought that he must be imagining things, but as they sat down at the tea table and he saw Cledra deliberately take a chair as far away from Eddie as possible, he knew that his intuition had been right and she was afraid.

To change her thoughts he suggested,

"I think, as you are the only lady present, Cledra, that pouring out the tea falls to you."

She looked at him a little shyly and then, obeying him without any arguing, changed her chair for the one in front of the silver tray with its large and beautifully chased silver teapot.

Eddie, helping himself to a sandwich, then said,

"Well, so far, so good. I am sure it is an anxiety off your mind, Lennox, that your grandmother and Miss Melford are now safely at The Hall."

The Earl frowned.

"It is my fault that I have forgotten to tell you, Eddie, although I have told all the servants, that the young lady staying with my grandmother is one of my cousins and is addressed as 'Miss Poyle'."

"You did forget me," Eddie complained, "but I certainly think it is a good idea for the name 'Melford' to be forgotten."

"You don't mind assuming my name?" the Earl asked, turning to Cledra.

She smiled at him.

"I am very – very honoured, but I hope you will tell me something of the history of my new – ancestors and especially about the flags that hang in the hall."

Before the Earl could reply, she added quickly,

"But perhaps you would find that boring. So instead could you tell me if there is in your library a history not only of the house but also of all those who have lived in it."

"I wonder if that would really interest you or if you are just being polite to its present owner?"

"I think history that is the most fascinating subject that anybody could possibly study," Cledra replied. "Mama and I used to read lots of history books together and Papa and I used to 'travel' all over the world with an Atlas and sometimes he would find pictures of the places on our route."

The way she spoke made the Earl aware that everything she had learnt in that way had been vividly real to her.

He thought it might be intriguing to take somebody who was so interested, but who had never travelled except in her mind, to the places that he himself had visited and enjoyed.

When he was young, he had travelled extensively because his father had felt that it was good for his education.

He wondered what Cledra would think of Venice, of Athens and of the Pyramids of Egypt, which he had climbed with his Tutor when he was only sixteen.

Then he told himself that her interest was only that of a schoolgirl who had nothing else to occupy her mind and, once she had discovered the Social world, the parties, the balls, Receptions and Assemblies, her horizons would be confined to Mayfair.

Because he was so silent, Cledra looked at him a little apprehensively and said in a very small voice,

"H-have I – said anything – wrong?"

"Why should you think that?" the Earl asked.

"You – you were looking scornful – and perhaps I am mistaken – cynical."

Eddie laughed.

"You will find when you know our host better, Miss Poyle, that this is his habitual expression and if he is bored he shows it!"

Cledra's eyes searched the Earl's face before she said,

"I am – sorry if I am being boring. Mama always told me that I should not – talk about myself – but you did ask me."

"I asked you and I wanted an answer," the Earl replied, "and I was not in the least bored with what you said. On the contrary it interested me enormously."

He glanced at Eddie on the other side of the table defiantly before he went on,

"I was in fact thinking how interesting it would be to take somebody like yourself who has been abroad only in her imagination to, let us say, Venice and watch their reaction."

"I think in most cases," Cledra said as if he had asked her a direct question, "the reality would be much more thrilling and satisfying than anything one could possibly imagine."

"Then you are admitting that there are limitations to one's imagination?"

"That entirely depends on the person," Cledra replied, "and then, of course, on how descriptive the books were they had read, or how well the place in question had been explained by somebody who had actually been there."

The Earl smiled.

He liked the logic behind Cledra's reasoning.

He also appreciated that she could think quickly and answer his questions in the same way that Eddie might have done when they were alone having dinner together.

Then aloud he said,

"I would like to make an experiment."

Cledra looked at him as he went on,

"I am wondering what you imagine my stables are like where a horse called 'Winged Victory' is housed at this moment. We might go now and see if the picture in your imagination is true to life."

A light came into Cledra's eyes that was almost dazzling.

"Can we really go and see St – Winged Victory now?" she asked, stumbling over the name. "I was longing to ask you if I could do so – but I was afraid you might think it – presumptuous of me to suggest it."

"I should have thought it very unnatural if you had bottled up your feelings very much longer," the Earl replied, "and shall I say that my intuition told me that was what you were longing for?"

She gave him a smile that was more expressive than anything she could have said and he rose to his feet.

"Come along then and as, I have no wish, if you are tired, to get into trouble with Hannah, I shall expect you to lie down before dinner."

"That is what Hannah said," Cledra answered, "but I did not think that you would ask me to dine with you."

"Eddie and I would be very disappointed if you did not do so," the Earl said, "but we can, of course, wait for another night."

"I will rest and please – please – may I dine with you? It will be very – very exciting for me – as I have never been to a dinner party before."

"Then Eddie and I will entertain you and I only hope you will not be disappointed."

"Nothing that – concerns you – could be – disappointing," Cledra answered.

CHAPTER SIX

They walked the short distance to the stable yard and the Earl deliberately went slowly so that it would not be too much for Cledra.

When they passed under the arch, surmounted by the Poynton Coat of Arms in stone, that led into the stables, Cledra saw that the buildings were architecturally unusually fine.

As she had expected, everything was meticulously clean and the cobbled yard seemed to glitter in the sunshine.

The Earl would have led the way to the first stable on the right, but Cledra paused, held up her hand and asked,

"May I show you how I can call – Winged Victory without using my – voice?"

The Earl replied,

"Of course. I am prepared for surprises from your horse!"

She gave him a little smile before she said,

"Then please would you ask one of the grooms just to open his stall and leave him to come out on his own?"

A groom had appeared as soon as the Earl had walked through the arch and now he received the directions that Cledra had asked for with some surprise, but hurried away to obey them.

They stood waiting and the Earl realised that Cledra was concentrating her thoughts on her horse, sending them towards him almost he thought like live vibrations.

Then from the door some way from them Winged Victory appeared.

He was not rushing out, as another horse might have done on being set free, but moving with dignity.

Without pausing he came straight towards Cledra.

She moved a few steps forward to greet him, her arms going out to him and he nuzzled his nose against her.

The Earl said nothing, but Eddie remarked in a low voice,

"They ought to be painted like that. I have never seen such an attractive picture."

The Earl did not reply, but he knew that what Eddie had said was right.

In her white gown with the sun glinting on her hair, her arms raised to Winged Victory's arched neck, Cledra together with her horse made a picture of such grace and beauty that it was difficult to decide which artist could do them justice.

Cledra was speaking softly,

"I have missed you so much. How are you, my dearest? Have they looked after you properly?"

There was no doubt that the horse was as pleased to see her as she was to see him.

Then, as if she suddenly remembered that the Earl was there, Cledra said,

"Now I want Winged Victory to thank you, as I have tried to do."

She moved away from the horse and gave him an order in a gentle voice that only he could hear.

First he bowed his head three times and then slowly he knelt on one leg in front of the Earl and put his head down in a posture that was part of the training in the Spanish Riding School.

For a moment he remained there and as he did so Cledra beside him dropped the Earl a deep curtsey.

"Thank you again," she murmured.

As they both rose, the Earl walked forward to pat Winged Victory, saying,

"I have never before been thanked so eloquently."

"Papa and I taught him when he was very young," Cledra explained, "and once he knows a trick he never forgets it."

"I congratulate you," Eddie interposed.

Cledra turned her head as he spoke and once again the Earl thought that there was an expression of fear in her eyes.

It would be difficult in the future, he thought, to make her forget that men could be cruel and frightening.

It was the same with a horse, once it has been ill-treated. It would remain nervous and restless for a long time.

His thoughts inevitably brought his mind back to the problem of what to do about Cledra, but deliberately he set it aside.

"I want, to show you my horses," he said aloud, "so perhaps you could persuade Winged Victory to go back to his stall while I do so. In any case I expect you want to see how he is housed."

"I know he will be comfortable in your stables," Cledra answered.

She walked towards the door that Winged Victory had emerged through and he moved beside her without there being any need for a bridle.

The Earl's stables were constructed in the traditional manner, each horse having a wooden stall with iron bars above it and a passage running in front of them down the whole building with windows onto the yard outside.

Although the design was very much the same as the stables belonging to her uncle, Cledra saw at once that in the Earl's there was more air and light and the stalls themselves were larger.

As she went into Winged Victory's stall, she could not help a little shudder of horror as she remembered how she had been beaten and tied up by her uncle.

Then, because she knew that it was childish to be frightened of what was past, she put her arms around Winged Victory and laid her cheek against him.

"You will be happy here, darling – and – safe."

She spoke little above a whisper not expecting the Earl to hear what she said, but he replied,

"I promise you he will be guarded by night and day and I have given orders for the horses' water never at any time to be left outside their stalls."

Cledra gave a little sigh of relief and replied,

"I knew – you would think of – everything."

As if he wanted to divert her thoughts, the Earl said in a different tone of voice,

"I hope you are not too tired. I want to show you a few of my horses that I hope you will think are the right type of companions for Winged Victory."

Cledra gave a little chuckle, which was what he had intended, as she replied,

"I promise you he is not a snob, but like an ambitious mother I want him to have 'nice friends'."

She made the Earl laugh at this and she thought, as she went down the passage beside him looking at the magnificent horseflesh he owned, that this was a happy place.

The grooms were smiling and she knew instinctively that they really cared for the horses and tended them not merely because they were paid to do so.

When they had walked the length of the first stable, the Earl stopped to say

"I have a great many more horses to show you, but not today. We shall both get into trouble with Hannah if you don't go and lie down as you promised to do."

"I would be very disappointed at having to go back now," Cledra replied, "if I was not looking forward to my first dinner party."

"Then you must try to sleep for at least an hour," the Earl suggested firmly.

"I will try and thank you for showing me such wonderful horses – I know they are as happy as Winged Victory is – now."

She turned away as she finished speaking and ran from the stable yard, disappearing through the stone arch at the end of it.

Eddie, who had been in a different stable from the Earl and Cledra, rejoined his host.

As they walked back towards the house, he said,

"I was tactful because it was quite obvious that your protégée wanted you to herself. You have made another conquest, Lennox!"

The Earl did not reply and Eddie went on,

"I suppose it is understandable, but I have a feeling that she is afraid of me simply because I am a man."

"I thought that myself," the Earl agreed.

"God knows she has every reason for it after the way she was treated by Melford," Eddie remarked. "It's a blessing that she is not afraid of you."

"I saved her and I saved her horse!" the Earl replied briefly.

"And that is all that matters for the moment," Eddie said as if he was following the line of his own thoughts, "but what about the future? She will have to get used to being with other people and men will find her extremely attractive."

There was a frown between the Earl's eyes as if he disliked discussing Cledra even with his closest friend.

But, as Eddie was obviously waiting for an answer, he said after a considerable pause,

"I think there is no point in trying to make decisions until we have some idea of what Melford's next attack will be."

"If you are expecting him to strike again," Eddie said quickly, "I hope we shall not have to wait too long. Quite frankly, Lennox, when I think of the crimes he has committed already, I feel extremely apprehensive as to what will happen next."

The Earl, although he did not say so, felt the same and, when he went upstairs to change for dinner, he said to Yates,

"There has been no sign of any strangers around the place or anybody making enquiries about Miss Cledra?"

Yates shook his head.

"No, my Lord. I've bin keepin' a careful watch, as your Lordship told me, but there's nobody new in the village. So I'm keepin' my fingers crossed and hopin' we've covered our tracks successfully."

"I doubt it," the Earl said under his breath as if he spoke to himself.

As he had his bath and dressed, he was thinking that there was nothing else he could do but wait.

He had doubled the nightwatchmen in the house and instructed his Head Groom that there must always be a stable boy on duty in each stable during the night.

There was really nothing else he could arrange without alarming everybody, which he thought would be a great mistake.

At the same time he had the uncomfortable feeling that Sir Walter was encroaching on them and would never rest until he had taken his revenge in some way or another on Cledra.

He was, however, determined not to express his anxiety aloud or to let either Yates or Eddie have any idea how worried he was.

When he went downstairs, it was to find that Eddie already waiting for him in the salon. For Cledra's benefit the Earl had ordered the tapers in the two great crystal chandeliers to be lit.

When a few minutes later she came into the room, he thought as she walked towards him that the gown he had chosen for her in London was a perfect frame for her fragile beauty.

It was a young girl's gown and therefore white, but it was skilfully embroidered with pearls and diamonds like dewdrops and the puffed sleeves and the décolletage were decorated with tiny frills of lace.

She moved, the Earl thought, with the same dignity and grace that had characterised Winged Victory and when she reached him she dropped him a little curtsey and then ingenuously, as if she could not hide her feelings, she exclaimed,

"This is very exciting. I have never worn such a beautiful – beautiful – gown as this!"

"I am glad it pleases you."

"It is so lovely that I feel as if it had been made by fairy fingers and should have been worn by Titania rather than me.

"I see you know your *Midsummer Night's Dream*," the Earl smiled.

"Of course and that is exactly what being here in this wonderful house is. I do hope I shall not – wake up too – quickly."

The Earl laughed.

While they were talking, Eddie had brought Cledra a glass of champagne.

Now, as he held it out to her, she took it from him, but was very careful, the Earl noticed, not to touch his fingers as she did so.

She also did not look at him as she said 'thank you' and having taken the glass moved a few steps further away from him.

When they went into dinner, the Earl sat at the top of the table in a high-backed chair with Cledra on his right and Eddie on his left.

Because when he exerted himself nobody could be more amusing or witty, the Earl started telling Cledra some of his more comical experiences on the Racecourse.

Soon she was laughing with sheer delight at the incidents he described and even looking at Eddie and listening to him when he tried to cap the Earl's stories with some of his own.

The food was delicious and the wines, although they did not interest Cledra, were superb.

Then, as dessert was on the table and the servants withdrew, she said,

"If all dinner parties are as delightful and amusing as this one, I hope I shall be invited to lots and lots of them."

She spoke spontaneously as a child might easily have done, but then she added in consternation,

"That sounds as if I am – imposing myself on – you and you know – that is something I don't – mean to do."

"What you said was a compliment," the Earl answered, "which I greatly appreciate and, as you are my guest, I want you to enjoy yourself."

"You know I am," she answered. "How could I help it when I am in a Fairy Palace, wearing a Fairy gown, and dining with a Prince?"

She looked at the Earl as she spoke and he thought that of all the compliments he had received this was the one he was most likely to remember.

At the same time he knew Cledra was not speaking to him with love but with gratitude and admiration, finding that he was the only safe, secure and inspiring factor in her life, which since the death of her father had been frightening and ugly.

It struck him that never before had he known a woman whose feelings for him had been so different from what he had learned to expect.

Women had always pursued him and striven with every wile and artifice to possess him.

But he had never before been in the position of protector, Guardian and saviour to a woman who could say the most flattering and admiring things to him without there being any note of passion in her voice or flicker of desire in her eyes.

Because Cledra was so different, the Earl found that the way she spoke and the way she looked at him intriguing.

He was also aware that she was intelligent and very much better educated than most women he had known.

He realised that it was because she had been so much with her father that she talked both to him and to Eddie quite naturally and on equal terms without any of the coyness that another woman would have shown on being alone with two attractive men.

"Tomorrow," the Earl declared, "when I have shown you the rest of the horses in my stable, I shall look forward to showing you some of the treasures in my house."

He saw as he spoke that Cledra's eyes lit up with delight.

"Will you really?" she asked. "Your grandmother has told me some of the history of the family and I want so much to see your pictures and your furniture, some of which she informed me came from France."

"Are you really interested?" the Earl asked.

So often in the past women had expressed an ardent desire to see the contents of his houses, but he had always discovered that it was really only a means of obtaining an invitation to stay.

Once they were comfortably ensconced in The Hall they made no effort to look at anything except himself.

"I am quite certain," Cledra said in answer to his question, "that the reality of what I shall see will be far more uplifting than my imagination and far more beautiful than the illustrations I have poured over in the past."

There was no doubt that she was speaking sincerely and the Earl thought that it would interest him to take her round and hear her comments on the pictures, which had been collected by his ancestors and to which he had added some very fine modern Masters.

He also had several rooms arranged by periods, so that there was a King Charles II Room, a Queen Anne Room and a George II Room, which contained both pictures and furniture that were finer than one could see anywhere else in the country.

He thought with a smile that Cledra would undoubtedly have something different to say about these from anything that he might have heard before.

"That is a promise," Cledra said, "and I shall not let you forget it."

"I always keep my promises," the Earl replied loftily.

"Of course you do," she agreed.

"Why do you say that so positively?"

She smiled.

"I should be very stupid," she replied, "if I did not know that you would not only keep your word because it is an honourable thing to do but also because you would never give anyone a promise lightly."

The Earl looked at her in surprise.

"I cannot understand why you should say that."

"She has been reading your character, Lennox," Eddie remarked, "and she is absolutely right. All the time I have known you, I have never heard you make a rash promise or you would do something that you have no intention of doing."

"It is the difference between being a positive person," Cledra interposed, "and somebody who cannot really be trusted."

"You are making me conceited," the Earl answered, "but I am glad you think that you can trust me."

"Yates has told me, as has your grandmother, how many people have trusted you – in the past and because they did so you saved their lives. And now you have saved – mine."

She spoke very softly and it was somehow very moving, but, because the Earl was somewhat embarrassed by his own reactions, he said,

"Shall we go into the salon? I see no reason for you to leave us, as would be, of course, correct."

Cledra gave a little cry.

"Should I have suggested it – already? I am sorry if I have made a – mistake."

"You have not made one," the Earl answered, "and it would be very foolish for you to sit alone in the salon when Eddie and I can drink our port and talk to you at the same time."

Cledra looked at him a little uncertainly, as if she was not sure whether he was just being kind to her and she had in point of fact made a social error.

Then, as he smiled at her reassuringly, she felt a little tremor go through her because he was so kind and she knew that she was safe while he was there.

*

The Earl did not allow Cledra to stay in the salon for long.

"This is your first night of gaiety," he said, "and I know that Hannah will be annoyed if I keep you up late."

He saw the disappointment in her eyes and he added,

"There is always tomorrow."

"You mean – I can dine with you – tomorrow night?"

"If you are not already bored with two old gentlemen like Eddie and myself!"

Cledra gave a little laugh.

"Now you are teasing me, for you know that I could never be bored with you. Being here and having such a wonderful dinner party has been the most exciting thing that has ever happened to me."

When she had said 'goodnight' and had gone upstairs, Eddie poured himself another glass of port from the decanter at his side as he said,

"She is entrancing! You. should talk to your grandmother and think of a way of finding her a suitable husband."

"A husband?" the Earl queried as if he had never heard of the species.

"You must be aware," Eddie replied, "that if Cledra, I cannot go on calling her 'Miss', is married, Melford would no longer have any jurisdiction over her."

The Earl looked surprised.

"I must say I had not thought of that."

"It's the obvious and simplest solution to your problem. Once she marries, Sir Walter can hardly beat her and, if he poisons her or her husband, he will undoubtedly hang for it!"

He paused for a moment before he added,

"The difficulty, of course, is going to be how you can introduce her to eligible bachelors without Melford becoming aware of it and trying to snatch her away or kill her, whichever is in his mind at this particular moment."

"I will take damned good care he does neither of those things," the Earl said harshly.

He rose to his feet as he spoke and walked across the room to the window.

He pulled back the curtain and looked out at the night. The sky was brilliant with stars and there was a half-moon rising above the trees in the Park.

It was so beautiful that it was hard to think that somewhere Sir Walter Melford, mad and thirsting for revenge, was planning some other dastardly action against him and he must be perpetually on his guard.

Just for a moment the Earl thought that he had been extremely lucky to have become involved in a situation that had nothing to do with him.

Then he was aware that it was not only a challenge but had brought him a new interest that had made him feel as if he had come alive in a manner that he had not known for several years.

Only when he was pitting himself against an enemy who was unpredictable as Sir Walter was, had he felt as he did now and the Earl knew it was something that, while in its way it was alarming, was also exhilarating and in an inexplicable way enjoyable.

Because the Earl had made no response to the solution he had offered and was also behaving in a manner that was somehow uncharacteristic, Eddie, who had not moved from the comfortable chair by the fireplace, was watching him closely.

There was a question in his eyes and he was perplexed by the Earl's behaviour.

Then after a moment there was a faint smile on his lips as he reached out towards his glass of port.

*

The Earl went to bed and lay for quite some time thinking about Cledra.

Almost as if he could see it happening again in front of his eyes, he saw the picture she had made in the stable yard as she had stood with her arms raised to Winged Victory and again when they had thanked him so gracefully for what he had done for them.

He was just drifting into a dreamless sleep when he heard the handle of his door turn and was instantly alert with the quickness of a man who was used to danger.

When the door opened, there was the light from a candle and he turned his head to see to his astonishment that Cledra had come into the room.

"What is it? What do you want?" he asked raising himself on his elbow to face her.

She walked right across the room, which was quite a large one, until she reached the side of the bed.

When he could see her face in the candlelight, her eyes were wide and very dark and frightened.

"What is it? the Earl asked again.

He knew, when there was a little pause before she answered, that she was finding it hard to find the words in which to reply.

"Y-you will think it very – f-foolish of me," she stammered after a moment, "but I know that – Winged Victory is – in d-danger."

Thinking that the Earl was going to tell her that she was talking nonsense she quickly went on,

"I-I cannot explain – but just as I can make him come to me without words – I know now that he is – calling out to me – and I h-have to go to him!"

The Earl looked at here in perplexity.

The he realised that she had dressed herself and was wearing her riding habit and he thought perhaps that it was the only dark clothing she possessed.

Without asking any more questions he made up his mind.

"If you think your horse is in danger, Cledra, we will go at once to the stables."

He saw the expression on Cledra's face change to one of relief and he knew how scared she must have been that he would not agree.

"You had better leave me your candle," the Earl suggested, "and wait outside the door. I imagine there is some light in the passage."

"Yes," Cledra agreed, "and – I will wait."

She put the candle down on the table beside his bed and walked back the way she had come.

Only as she reached the door did the Earl say,

"It might be a good idea to wake Eddie. Just knock on his door and say I want him."

Cledra did not turn round, but he knew by the way her body stiffened that it was something she had no wish to do, so he added,

"Never mind, I will do it as soon as I have dressed. I will not be more than a few minutes."

The door closed behind her and the Earl jumped out of bed.

Because he was quite capable of dressing himself as quickly, if not quicker, than when Yates was with him, it was only two minutes before he opened the door and found as he expected that Cledra was waiting in the passage just outside.

The candles in the sconces had guttered low so that it was obviously much later than he had thought, but there was enough light for him to see the expression on her face and he knew that she was straining with every nerve in her body to beg him to hurry.

She was convinced in a way that it was difficult to understand that Winged Victory was actually in danger.

The Earl did not speak. He just walked across the passage and opened the door of the room where Eddie was sleeping.

He reached the bed and shook him by the shoulder.

"Wake up, Eddie!" he called out. "Cledra thinks that something is happening in the stables and we are going there at once. Follow as quickly as you can."

Eddie did not argue, he merely started to climb out of bed and by the time he had done so the Earl was back in the passage and with Cledra beside him walked towards the centre of the house.

He was thinking as he did so that it would be a mistake to alert the nightwatchman until he was quite certain that Cledra's instinct was correct.

He had been very careful since her arrival at The Hall to impress upon Hannah and Yates that they must not talk of there being any danger that concerned his guest and he thought now that to rush the servants from the house to the stables unless there was real necessity for it might do more harm than good.

'Whatever is happening,' he told himself confidently, 'I feel sure that Eddie and I can cope with it.'

When they reached the top of the main staircase, where there was a footman on duty and doubtless a nightwatchman in the process of making his rounds, the Earl moved straight on down the passage to a secondary staircase.

Without wasting time in politeness he went down the staircase first, moving swiftly and knowing that as far as Cledra was concerned nothing could be swift enough.

It was only a short distance to a door that was bolted, but which led out of the side of the house from where it was but a short distance to the arch that was the entrance to the stables.

It was as the archway was silhouetted against the starlit sky and the Earl had to slow his pace because the path between the shrubs was in darkness that he felt Cledra's hand slip into his.

He knew from the way that her fingers trembled that she was frightened and he knew too that she was trusting him and depending on him in a way that made him feel determined that he would not fail her.

While he had not wanted to raise a general alarm, nevertheless, as he left his bedroom, he had put a pistol into the pocket of his coat, which he had previously primed.

They reached the arch and, as they stepped into the stable yard, the Earl thought that everything was quiet and as it should be.

Then he heard a horse neighing in fear, which instantly was taken up by other horses, and there was the sound of animals moving restlessly in their stalls.

Cledra's fingers tightened on his and she gave a little cry of horror.

"Fire!"

Even as she spoke, the Earl saw a red light coming from the window of a stable and knew that it came from the direction of Winged Victory's stall.

"*Fire!*"

He could not only see it but thought that he could smell it and he took his hand from Cledra's and started to run towards the door of the stable that Winged Victory had emerged from that morning, shouting as he did so at the top of his voice,

"Fire! *Fire!*"

By the time his cry seemed to echo back at him he had reached the outer door of the stable and pulled it open.

As he did so, there was a loud explosion and the noise from the horses was suddenly deafening.

He saw the stall where Winged Victory was housed was alight with flames and the horse was rearing, bucking and neighing with terror.

It took the Earl only a second to reach the door that led into Winged Victory's stall.

He pulled it open and saw as he did so that it was not bolted as it should have been.

Then, as smoke and flames made it difficult to see what was happening, he realised that the horse was unable to turn round because it was wearing a bridle and had been roped to the manger.

The hay in the manger was alight and so was the straw on the ground on which Winged Victory was bucking frantically in his efforts to pull himself free.

The Earl recognised the danger from the horse's hoofs and he was about to try to insert himself between the plunging animal and the wall to get to his head when Cledra was there before him.

When the Earl would have put out his hands to stop her, it was too late.

She was already in the stall speaking to Winged Victory quietly and calmly.

She had reached her horse's head and pulled off the bridle and, as he turned round and rushed out through the open door, she was left standing silhouetted against the flames.

The Earl reached her, picked her up in his arms and as he did so was aware that there was the body of a man lying on the floor at the back of the stall.

It was difficult to see clearly in the flames now leaping higher and higher from the blazing straw and the hay in the manger, but, as the Earl carried Cledra out into the yard, there was an explosion behind them and he knew who lay there.

As he looked down at Cledra, concerned only with her, he was aware that somebody was slapping his shoulders to put out the flames that were burning his coat and that his forehead was hurting him.

But he was sure since she had hidden her face against his shoulder as he lifted her up in his arms that the flames had not touched her face.

Then Eddie was asking her,

"Are you all right?"

By now the grooms, appearing from every direction, had rushed into the stables to release the other horses trapped amongst the flames.

The Earl set Cledra down on a mounting block and, putting his hand under her chin, turned her face up to his so that he could see by the light of the moon that she was uninjured.

As he did so, Winged Victory was beside them and the horse was nuzzling at Cledra who put up her hands weakly to touch him.

"You are both safe," the Earl declared quietly and went back to the stables to help release the remainder of the horses.

Grooms were now carrying buckets of water to put out the fire and the horses, frightened but safe, were careering about the cobbled yard.

"Turn them into the paddock," the Earl ordered sharply and several of the stable boys hurried to obey him, while the rest strove to extinguish the flames.

Already half the building was ablaze and the stall where it had started was an inferno, with more explosions coming from it.

Only after the roof had fallen in was the estate fire engine brought from the shed where it was kept.

It was a new acquisition that had never been used and both the Head Groom and the Earl had forgotten it until the traditional manner of putting out fire with buckets passed from hand to hand had been put into operation.

When finally the fire engine was in use, the fire had destroyed half the stalls in that stable, but the rest were intact and comparatively undamaged.

The horses were all safe, if shocked and restless.

The Earl had them brought one by one from the paddock and housed in empty stables on the other side of the yard where they were given a good feed.

He ordered that each one be covered by a blanket to keep them warm for the rest of the night and it was only when everybody had obeyed him and peace had been more or less restored that he went back to where he had left Cledra.

She was still sitting on the mounting block and Winged Victory was beside her, apparently quite calm after his ordeal and unhurt expect where the front of his mane had been singed and so in places had his neck.

The Earl was aware that, because Cledra was talking to him and caressing him, he was quiet, while the other horses who had suffered much less were still upset and would doubtless be restless for several days.

He stood watching Cledra for a moment before she was aware that he was there.

Then he said,

"I have a stable ready, if you can persuade Winged Victory to go into it."

"I am sure he will – if I go with him," Cledra answered.

She rose to her feet and, as the Earl led the way, she walked beside him with Winged Victory following her.

He had deliberately chosen a stall that was not only on the opposite side of the yard, but as far away as possible from where the fire had taken place.

It had not been used for some time and the grooms had already put down fresh straw and filled the manger with hay and there was also a good feed of oats like that being distributed amongst the other horses.

The Head Groom was waiting and had a blanket ready to throw over Winged Victory's back.

At first he would not let the man touch him and then, when Cledra helped and talked to him, he was quiet except that his ears twitched and now he was in a stall he seemed nervous and apprehensive.

"It's all right," Cledra said in a soothing voice, "I promise you, dearest, it is all right. You are quite – safe now – and you shall never be – hurt again."

The Head Groom moved out of the stall and Cledra turned to the Earl,

"I think perhaps I had better stay with him."

"I am sure that is unnecessary, but, if you can persuade him to eat, he will be all right."

Cledra put some oats in the palm of her hand and, although at first he was reluctant, she finally persuaded Winged Victory to take a small amount and then to eat from the manger.

"He will be fine now," the Earl said. "I am going to insist that you go to bed."

Cledra moved nearer to him.

Then she muttered in a small voice,

"S-suppose – Uncle Walter comes back and – tries again?"

"He will not do that," the Earl replied.

"How can you be – sure?"

"Because he is dead!"

Cledra's eyes opened wide and she stared at the Earl as if she could hardly believe what she had heard.

"H-how do you – know that?"

"He was lying on the floor in Winged Victory's stall," the Earl answered. "I saw him as I carried you out."

She looked at him incredulously and he went on,

"I think I know what happened, your uncle was determined to burn down the stables, which he would have done if you had not sensed that there was danger. The stable boy who was on guard had been found. He had received a blow on the head, which rendered him unconscious."

Cledra gave a little murmur, but she did not speak and the Earl continued,

"Your uncle then went into Winged Victory's stall, put on his bridle and tied him to the manger just as he tied you."

Cledra gave a cry and the Earl carried on,

"But Winged Victory did not submit so tamely. He must have reared up and knocked your uncle down. At the same time the candle lantern he carried that he intended to set the place on fire with was knocked over."

"How could he do such – a horrible thing?" Cledra gasped.

"The straw flared up," the Earl went on, "igniting some fireworks that your uncle was carrying and which I think he intended to throw about the stables, inciting the other horses to madness."

Cledra closed her eyes as the Earl said angrily,

"As I heard them exploding, I realised that they were part of your uncle's diabolical plot to destroy not only Winged Victory but all my horses as well!"

"How could he think of anything so cruel — so *wicked*?" Cledra asked in a broken voice.

Now, as if the horror of it was too much to bear she hid her face against the Earl's shoulder.

He put his arms around her saying,

"You have been through too much already. I will tell you the rest tomorrow, but I want you to know for certain that Winged Victory will be quite safe tonight. And so will you."

As he spoke, he saw that she was crying and, lifting her up in his arms, he carried her out of the stall and across the stable yard towards the house.

CHAPTER SEVEN

Cledra came back to consciousness and felt that she must have been sleeping for a hundred years.

She could hear Hannah moving softly about the room and thought that she had heard her earlier. She vaguely remembered too being given something sweet and soothing to drink before she had drifted away again into a dreamless sleep.

Now, with what was an effort, she opened her eyes and saw the sunshine streaming in through the windows

Hannah came to the bedside to ask,

"Are you awake, miss?"

As she spoke, the terror of the fire came to Cledra's mind and she cried out in a voice that did not sound like her own.

"The – horses! Winged Victory! He is – all right?"

"Perfectly all right, miss," Hannah replied soothingly. "In fact I'm sure it was your horse I sees his Lordship ridin' not an hour since as he galloped across the Park."

"His Lordship was – riding Winged Victory?" Cledra said slowly, as if she was saying it to herself rather than to Hannah.

"I'm sure I'm right," Hannah insisted, "and, when his Lordship comes back, he'll be right glad to hear you're awake. He's bin askin' after you every day."

"Every – *day*?"

Hannah smiled.

"Yes, miss, you've been sleepin' for three days and t'was the best thing you could possibly do to get over the shock of it all."

"Did you say – three days?" Cledra asked, finding it hard to understand what Hannah was saying and thinking that she must be very stupid.

"Yes, three days, miss, and now they're clearin' up the stables and his Lordship's havin' fire drill inside the house and out."

As Hannah was talking, she was patting the pillow behind Cledra's head and then she said,

"I'm goin' downstairs now to fetch you somethin' to eat, miss. You'll be hungry after sleepin' for so long."

"How could – I have slept for – three days?"

"That's a question you'll have to ask Mr. Yates," Hannah replied. "But his sleepin' herbs as he calls them will do you no harm and both he and his Lordship wanted you first and foremost to get over the shock."

Cledra drew in her breath, thinking of how frightened she had been, and remembering that the Earl had told her that her uncle was dead.

Hannah had gone from the room and looking at the sunshine Cledra thought that now everything was light and there was no dark menace to make her afraid and anxious.

Then almost as if somebody gave her a blow she was aware that now she was free of her uncle there would be no reason for her to stay here and, as an uninvited guest, she would have to make plans to leave.

Suddenly she felt frantic at the idea.

'Where can I go?'

'What can I do?'

'Who will want me?'

The questions seemed to tumble over themselves in her mind and, because she was unprepared for them, she could see herself riding away from the great house on Winged Victory and going out through the lodge gates into a huge, frightening and empty world where nobody would care what became of her.

Then, as she felt the fear of the future rising in her breast, she knew that when she had gone she would never see the Earl again and would have lost her only safety and security.

'What can I do?'

It was only on her account that he had left London at the height of the Season and come to the country so that he could protect her and his horses from her uncle.

Now he could return to his parties of the beautiful women who loved him.

Her uncle was dead and Cledra found it impossible to be anything but glad. He had been evil and mad.

Yet, because of what she had suffered at his hands and because too, as an orphan, she was alone in the world, she knew that only with the Earl could she feel safe and secure.

She sat up in bed.

'I must not – impose upon him,' she told herself, 'and now that he need no longer be afraid of what Uncle Walter will do next, he will – certainly not – want me.'

She felt as if what she was thinking was like a dagger in her heart and she threw herself back against the pillows and hiding her face she began to cry.

*

The Earl on returning from riding was informed by the butler that there was a gentleman to see him in his study.

"It's a Mr. Harriman, my Lord."

Handing his hat, riding gloves and whip to a footman, the Earl replied,

"I am indeed expecting him."

A man with greying hair and spectacles rose hurriedly to his feet as the Earl entered the study.

"I received your communication, my Lord," he said, "and came here from London immediately."

The Earl seated himself and indicated a chair opposite him.

"When I learned that you are the Solicitors in charge of Sir Walter Melford's affairs," he began, "I wished to talk to you before you approached Miss Melford."

"We were in fact searching for Miss Melford," Mr. Harriman replied, "and, when we were told by your Lordship's secretary that she was staying here, the information saved us a great deal of anxiety."

Mr. Harriman spoke in the slow precise manner that was characteristic of his profession and the Earl's voice in contrast sounded quick and alert as he replied,

"Miss Melford has not been well and, as I wish to spare her any unnecessary legal difficulties, I suggest that you communicate first to me what her position is now that Sir Walter Melford, who was her Guardian, is dead."

Mr. Harriman opened the briefcase he held on his knees.

"My partners and I thought that your Lordship would like a concise statement of Sir Walter's affairs and how they affect his niece. I think, my Lord, you will not be surprised to learn that she is now a very considerable heiress."

There was a distinct pause before the Earl responded,

"It is actually a great surprise. I rather expected that Sir Walter might not have included Miss Melford in his will."

"Sir Walter made his will fifteen years ago when he married," Mr. Harriman replied.

"Sir Walter was married? I had no idea!" the Earl exclaimed.

Mr. Harriman's thin lips twisted in a somewhat wry smile,

"Very few people were aware of it, my Lord, because it was a marriage that was kept secret even from his relatives and after the honeymoon abroad Lady Melford left him."

The Earl thought that this was not surprising, but said nothing.

"She returned to her family and my partners and I have always understood that she and Sir Walter never communicated with each other again except through our firm."

Again the Earl thought that this was understandable seeing what type of man Sir Walter had been.

Aloud he asked,

"But the will was not changed?"

"No, my Lord, although Sir Walter talked about it, nothing was done and in it provision was made for his wife, who is now dead, and everything else he possessed was left to his immediate heirs, who he expected to be his children."

The Earl did not speak and after a moment's pause Mr. Harriman continued,

"As your Lordship must be aware, Sir Walter's brother, Colonel Melford and his wife died two years ago and his only immediate heir, therefore, is Miss Cledra."

The Earl sat back in his chair.

This certainly, he thought, solved Cledra's problems from a financial point of view.

But he was wondering how she would manage to cope with considerable wealth and a large estate.

As if he read his thoughts Mr. Harriman said,

"Your Lordship, of course, knows Sir Walter's house and stables at Newmarket, but the family mansion in Sussex is very much larger and stands in two thousand acres of good agricultural land. There is also a house in Park Street in London."

"And you are telling me that there is nobody except Miss Melford to inherit this property and the money that goes with it?" the Earl asked.

He was thinking as he spoke that Sir Walter had just before his death received a great deal of money from the sale of his horses.

Mr Harriman turned over several papers before he replied,

"My partners and I, my Lord, have ascertained that there are a few quite distant relatives of Sir Walter and Miss Cledra, but the majority of them are elderly and in comfortable circumstances."

He inspected a document before he continued,

"Strangely enough there appear to be no young people in the family and it is in fact sad that Sir Walter had no children, while his brother, the popular and charming Colonel Melford, had only one daughter."

"I agree with you," the Earl replied, "and it is always a mistake for a young woman to be an heiress."

"You are quite right, my Lord," Mr. Harriman agreed. "London is full of the most undesirable fortune-hunters, as I and my partners have learnt from too many difficult and unsavoury Law suits."

The Earl rose to his feet.

"I am sure, Mr. Harriman, that you would like some refreshment and a rest before you return to London. I regret that Miss Melford is not well enough to see you, but I will give her any papers you may wish to leave with me."

He paused before he added,

"As soon as she is better I will either bring her to London where you can communicate with her at my house or I must ask you once again to make the journey here."

"I am very grateful to your Lordship," Mr. Harriman said, "and there is no great hurry, except as regards the investing of quite large amounts of money that are at the moment deposited in the Bank."

The Earl rang a gold bell that stood on his desk and, as the door opened, he held out his hand to the Solicitor who had placed a pile of papers on the desk.

"Thank you again, Mr. Harriman, for coming to see me and being so explicit. I will explain everything that you have told me to Miss Melford as soon as it is possible."

Mr. Harriman bowed.

"I can only thank your Lordship," he murmured respectfully.

When the Earl was alone he walked across the room to stand for a moment looking out at the sunshine in the garden, but he did not see the lilac and syringa coming into flower or the white doves flying overhead that had always been the delight of his grandmother.

Instead he was seeing the fear in Cledra's eyes when she looked at Eddie and remembering the way that she had instinctively moved a little closer to himself and seeking his protection.

'How the devil can she cope with two estates and a huge amount of money?' he reflected.

Because he did not know the answer, he went up the stairs to see his grandmother.

She was seated in the window of the sitting room which adjoined her bedroom and the sunshine was glittering on her jewels.

As the Earl approached her, her eyes to shine seemed almost as brightly as her diamonds.

"I have been waiting to see you, Lennox," she began as he crossed the room to lift her hand to his lips. "Eddie tells me that a Solicitor has called. I am sure that he has come to tell you how much that horrible man, Melford, has left and if any of it is for poor little Cledra."

The Earl laughed as he sat down beside the Countess.

"Is there anything that goes on in this house that you don't know about?" he enquired.

"Very little," the Countess admitted. "It would be very boring for me otherwise, tied here to my chair, and being unable to take part in the dramas which fill your life."

"Which I can well do without!"

"Nonsense!" the Countess exclaimed. "You know full well you enjoyed every moment of the fire that madman started."

The Earl did not contradict her, knowing that there was more than a grain of truth in what she was saying.

Nevertheless he hoped never again to go through the agonies he had suffered when he had thought that first Winged Victory and then Cledra would be burned to death.

It was an intense satisfaction to know that apart from the damage to his stable and the death of Sir Walter, nobody else had been badly hurt.

As if she followed his thoughts, the Countess looked at the scar on his forehead, which was healing, and said,

"That wound on most handsome men would be a disaster, but it gives you a raffish appearance and is actually quite becoming!"

"Thank you, Grandmama," the Earl replied somewhat wryly, "but may I inform you that it hurt abominably for the first forty-eight hours after it happened and the burns on my left hand are still extremely painful."

"That is what you must expect if you will play the hero," his grandmother replied unsympathetically. "I heard how you carried Cledra to safety and, of course, it was only because you went to the stables when she asked you to that her horse and many of yours were not destroyed."

"I am quite prepared to take some of the credit," the Earl replied, "but the person you must congratulate on having an infallible instinct for danger is Cledra."

"I will certainly tell her that when I see her," the Countess answered. "I hear she is awake."

"I think it was a good idea for her, as Yates prescribed, to sleep it off," the Earl replied, "and I certainly did not want her to be awake when I had what remained of her uncle sent to Sussex for burial in the family tomb."

He smiled as he continued,

"Her horse was restless and upset the next day, which would undoubtedly have perturbed her a great deal more."

"The horse is all right now?" the Countess enquired.

"Perfectly, I rode him this morning and there is nothing wrong except he will have to grow some new hair on his forehead and there are still some burnt patches on his nose and neck."

"And what about your own horses?"

"Settling down, although God knows what they would have been like if Melford had been able to throw his fireworks amongst them as he intended."

"Well, we need not think about him anymore," the Countess said, "but I am wondering what you are going to do about Cledra."

"That is what is worrying me because, Grandmama, her uncle's Solicitor has informed me that she inherits everything he left and he was a very rich man."

"Considering the way he treated her it is poetic justice," the Countess commented sharply.

"I agree. At the same time how can that child cope on her own? I suppose the first thing we shall have to do is to find her a chaperone."

"Or a husband!"

The Earl did not reply and the Countess was aware that he was frowning.

After what was quite a long silence she asked him, "You don't think that is a good idea?"

"I suppose it's a possible one," the Earl replied, "it is just that I am aware that at the moment Cledra would not feel at ease with strange men. Her uncle's treatment has left scars on her mind as well as on her body."

"Then the solution is obvious, dear boy."

"What is it?" the Earl enquired.

"You must look after her until you can find her a man she will accept," his grandmother replied, "and of whom she will not be afraid."

*

"I cannot go on sleeping!" Cledra exclaimed.

"No, of course not, miss," Hannah agreed, "and his Lordship's sent you a message."

"What is it?"

"He says when you feel strong enough he'd like to see you."

"Oh, Hannah! Why did you not tell me sooner? I will go downstairs and see him – at once."

"His Lordship's gone out, miss, and when he spoke to me he suggested if it was not too much for you, he'd like you to take tea with him in the Orangery."

"Of course it will not be too much for me."

Because she was excited at the idea Cledra ate her luncheon without argument and then allowed Hannah to settle her down for a short rest with the blinds half-drawn to keep out the sunshine.

She had no wish to sleep, wanting rather to think of the Earl and of how exciting it would be to see him again.

'I want him to talk to me,' she thought, 'I want him to tell me about Winged Victory and hear that all the other horses are unharmed,'

When Hannah came to pull up the blinds and help her to get dressed, she felt as if she wanted to dance.

But actually her legs felt a little unsteady after being in bed for so long.

However, when she was dressed in one of the lovely gowns that the Earl had brought her from London, she looked at herself in the mirror and thought that she would have been untruthful if she had not admitted that she looked very pretty.

She had grown thinner and her eyes were enormous in her face. There was a slight flush on her cheeks and her hair seemed to catch the sunlight.

"Now don't do too much, miss," Hannah admonished, "and if you feel tired come straight back to bed. I'll have everythin' ready for you."

"I am hoping his Lordship will ask me – down to dinner."

"It'll be too much for you and you'd much better stay quietly up here."

"That would be very dull," Cledra replied, "and, if his Lordship asks me to dine with him – I shall accept."

She did not wait for Hannah to say anything more, but hurried from the bedroom along the passage and down the great staircase.

The footman in the hall smiled as she appeared and she smiled back, thinking that the whole house seemed to welcome her as if she had been away for a long time.

Then, as she sped on towards the Orangery, she found herself hoping and even saying a little prayer that Eddie Lowther would not be there.

'I want to talk to the Earl alone,' Cledra thought, 'and it will spoil everything if there is anybody with him.'

She reached the Orangery and was assailed by the fragrance of the flowers and the sunshine pouring in all along the side of the building.

Then her heart gave a leap and turned a somersault as she had her first glimpse of the Earl standing at the open window waiting for her.

It was impossible not to run towards him and, when she reached him, she held out both her hands spontaneously in the sheer joy of seeing him again.

Then she gave a cry of horror.

"You have been – injured! Why did nobody – tell me?"

She was looking at the scar on his forehead and, as she saw that his left hand was bandaged, she exclaimed before he could speak,

"You have been badly – burnt! It must be very painful. Oh, I am sorry – I am so very – very sorry."

She held on to him as she spoke, one hand clinging to hi and, the other on his arm.

"My wounds are healing," the Earl answered with a smile, "and I promise you they now hardly hurt me at all."

"It is all my fault – and you might have been very badly injured."

There was a little sob in her voice and the Earl said quickly,

"I refuse to make a fuss about such trifles and let me tell you that Winged Victory has been very brave."

"He is – all right?"

"Perfectly."

"Hannah told me that you were riding him – today."

"And Winged Victory told me," the Earl smiled, "that he was looking forward to carrying you on his back."

"May I ride him tomorrow?"

"I hope you will be well enough."

Cledra's face was radiant and as if she was suddenly aware that she was still holding on to the Earl with both hands, she freed herself and said,

"Shall I pour out your – tea?"

"I am waiting for you to do so."

Cledra looked at the table and saw with a feeling of delight that there were only two cups.

She sat down and poured from a large silver teapot, the Earl watching her all the while.

When he took his cup from her, he said,

"I have a great deal to tell you, Cledra. Your uncle's Solicitor came here this morning."

Cledra did not reply, she merely looked up at him and the Earl could see the anxiety in her eyes.

"It was a surprise to me," he went on, "and I expect it will be somewhat of a surprise to you to know that everything your uncle possessed is now yours."

Cledra stared at him as if she could not believe that she had heard aright.

Then she cried,

"I don't want his – money! I will not – take it!"

The Earl did not speak and after a moment she added,

"Uncle Walter always taunted me by saying that he was leaving me to starve because – he intended to marry and have a son."

"But he did not do so," the Earl pointed out quietly.

"I *hate* his money, I will not touch it or anything he owned," Cledra suddenly raged.

Then after a little silence she said in a different tone,

"Except – please could we send some of it – at once to the old pensioners at Newmarket?"

The Earl smiled.

"I was right!" he exclaimed.

"Right?"

"I knew that would be the first thing you would think about and I have already sent a letter to my Manager at Newmarket instructing him to provide them with food and extra money until you can put their pensions on a proper legal basis."

Cledra gave a little cry.

"Oh, thank you! Only – you could be so – wonderful and so understanding. Thank you. I cannot bear to think that they should – suffer any – longer from Uncle Walter's – meanness and cruelty."

"I quite understand," the Earl said, "that, when you have provided for those who rely on you, you will want to sell the house at Newmarket, but your grandfather's house, which should have been your father's, is also yours."

"It was – home until Mama and I had to – live in a tiny – cottage," Cledra said almost beneath her breath.

"Your uncle was a wicked man and made many innocent people suffer," the Earl declared. "You will have to make up for his deficiencies."

"He would have – killed Winged Victory," Cledra said in a low voice.

"Winged Victory was fighting to save himself," the Earl answered, "and he certainly saved me from committing murder!"

Cledra put out her hand as if to hold onto him as she said,

"If you had – murdered Uncle Walter you might have been in terrible – trouble – and I would never have – forgiven myself because it would have been – my fault for coming to – you in the first place."

"But, as you have just said, Winged Victory saved me from that and it was your intuition that saved him and my horses from an appalling death."

"Winged Victory told me he was in danger," Cledra answered, "but, when I was thinking about it this morning, I knew it was very wonderful of you to – believe me. Most people, I am sure, would have thought that I was just being – hysterical."

"That is something you have never been in all the dramatic experiences that we have endured together," the Earl said, "and I want to tell you, Cledra, that I think you are very brave and a very exceptional young woman."

He liked the look of surprise in Cledra's eyes at his words and knew that she had not anticipated for a moment that he would praise her so fulsomely.

The colour flared into her cheeks as she asked,

"Do you – really mean – that?"

"I always say what I mean and I think that your father, if he was alive, would be very proud of you."

"Papa would have – understood as – you did."

Then she added in a different tone of voice,

"Now that Papa is dead surely there should be somebody like him or Grandpapa to live in the Big House. It has belonged to the Melfords for over a hundred years."

"As it is now yours," the Earl replied, "you will be able to live in it when you are married and carry on the family tradition."

Cledra stared at him for a moment and then she looked away out through the window into the garden.

"I-I shall – never marry," she sighed.

The Earl thought that this was what he might have expected her to feel and he said,

"You think that now because of the abominable way your uncle treated you. But you are young, Cledra, and you will find you will soon forget the horrors of these last two years."

She did not answer and after a moment he went on,

"When you are feeling stronger, we must make plans with my grandmother for you to meet the Social world in London and be presented to the Prince Regent at Buckingham Palace."

The Earl spoke very quietly with an almost coaxing note in his voice, but Cledra jumped to her feet.

"*No!*" she cried. "No. I will – not do that – and I know why you are – suggesting it! It is so that I shall meet men who will propose – marriage to me."

She quivered as she spoke and the Earl saw the fear that had been there before was back in her eyes.

He too rose to his feet.

"You must try to be sensible about this, Cledra. There is no hurry and we will talk it over when you feel stronger."

Cledra gave a little cry like an animal that has been trapped.

"I-I understand what you are – saying and I know, now that Uncle Walter is – dead, I have to go – away and not bother you any m-more. But I am frightened – and I will not know how to look after – myself when I am all – *alone*."

Her voice broke on the last word and, without thinking and without meaning to, she turned towards the Earl and flung herself against him hiding her face in his shoulder.

"H-how can I – I leave you?"

Her voice was choked with sobs and he could see tears running down her cheeks.

"I-I am only – safe when I am with – you."

Slowly his arms went round her.

He could feel that her sobs had become a tempest shaking her whole body.

"You must not cry," he urged her gently. "You have been so brave."

"I am – not b-brave," Cledra replied, "I am a – coward and I wish now I had – d-died. Then at least I would have – Papa and Mama to – look after me."

The Earl's arms tightened.

"You are not to say such things."

"H-how can I – help it if I have to go away all – alone and leave you?"

Her words were almost incoherent, but the Earl heard them.

"Do you mind so much leaving me?" he asked very gently.

"I-I – love you! I – love you because you are – so wonderful – so m-magnificent – and when I have gone you will forget me – just as you have forgotten all those – other women who – loved you, b-but I shall never – never – never forget you."

The Earl moved and put his hand under Cledra's chin to turn her face up to his.

She did not resist him. She merely closed her eyes against the light, the tears were still running down her cheeks and her lips trembled.

The Earl looked down at her for a long moment before he asked,

"Are you quite sure that you love me?"

"H-how can I – help it? There is – nothing else in the – whole world – but *you*."

Her voice broke again and the Earl bent his head and his lips were on hers.

For a moment Cledra could hardly believe what was happening to her and then his mouth seemed to take possession of her.

His lips were strong and demanding and she felt an ecstasy that was like a shaft of sunlight rising up through her body, sweeping away her misery and moving from her breasts into her throat.

It was so lovely, so rapturous and so unlike any other feeling that she had ever known before that she wished she might die while she knew such happiness and would therefore not lose it when he let her go.

Then the feeling seemed to intensify until it became alive and she knew that she had loved him from the first moment she had seen him and it was true when she said that he filled her whole life and there was nothing else.

The Earl's lips had at first been very gentle, then, as he felt the softness and sweetness of Cledra's, the ecstasy rising within her aroused the same feeling within himself.

His kisses became more intense and he held her closer still until he could feel her heart beating against his.

Only when he raised his head to look down at the radiance in her eyes did Cledra say a little incoherently,

"I – love you! *I love – you*! I knew that – if you kissed – me you would – take me into Heaven."

The Earl did not answer.

He merely kissed her again and now with a passion that made Cledra feel as if he was giving her the sun and its rays burnt their way into her heart.

She knew that whether he wanted her or not she was his, now and for all Eternity and, when he left her, he would take her heart and her soul with him and she would become but a shadow of herself, empty and alone.

But for the moment there was the rapture of being close to him, the wonder of his kisses and the feeling that she was safe and secure.

It was so glorious and so utterly perfect that she knew the vibrations between them made them one person and they were indivisible.

'How can I – lose him?' she asked herself desperately.

Then, because he was holding her, it was impossible to think of anything but that he was there and she was his and that he filled not only her whole world but the sky as well.

Only when the feelings he gave her were so intense that they were almost a physical pain did she break under the unendurable glory of it and hide her face against his neck.

"I-I – love you!" she whispered, "but I did not – know that l-love was like this."

"Like what?" the Earl asked and his voice sounded hoarse and unsteady.

"Like being in the sky – far away from – the world being safe and so unbelievably – gloriously happy that I think I must have – died."

"You are very much alive, my darling."

As if surprised at his words and the way he spoke, she raised her face to look up at him.

"P-please – say that again," she whispered, "just once because – I want to be sure I – heard it."

The Earl gave a little laugh.

"There are many things I want to say to you besides 'my darling', but, because you are intelligent, you must know that I love you as you love me."

"It – it cannot be – true!"

There was still a touch of tears in Cledra's voice.

He smiled before he replied,

"That is what I said when I found myself thinking that I could not lose you. You will stay with me so that I can look after you and I will not allow you to marry anybody but me!"

"Do you – really mean that you – want to *marry* me?"

"I think that is a sensible procedure when two people love each other as much as we do."

"You – love me? You really – love me?"

"I love you and I will persuade you to believe me, but it is going to take a long time."

Cledra gave a sound that was indescribable before she breathed,

"I never thought you would feel like that when there are so many – other women in your life – but I prayed that I could – stay with you just for a – little while because only with you can I – feel safe."

"I will keep you safe for ever," the Earl insisted, "and of one thing you can be sure, you will never leave me and I will *never* leave you."

"B-but – I may – bore you?"

"I was bored in the past because I had not found you. But now we have found each other, my adorable one, all we have to do is to keep loving each other."

"That is what I want to do for ever – and ever. And I will try in every way – possible to make you – happy."

"I *am* happy," the Earl said, "if that is the meaning of the extraordinary sensation I am feeling at the moment and I promise you, my darling, it is a very different feeling from any I have ever known before in my life."

Cledra lifted her lips to his.

"Kiss me – please – kiss me again," she asked. "I am so – afraid that this is all a – wonderful dream – and the Fairy Palace, the Fairytale gowns and you will all – disappear when I wake up."

"Which is the most important?" the Earl quizzed her.

"You! As long as you are there – everything else can go. I just want – you."

There was a passion in Cledra's voice that had not been there before and it made him aware how deeply she was feeling and he knew unbelievably and incredibly that he felt the same.

He had known, he felt, from the very beginning when Cledra had turned to him for help and protection that she was not only his responsibility but an essential part of him that he could not deny.

It was what he had been looking for all his life, although he had not been aware of it.

Now, because she was so helpless and at the same time so brave and, because she had given him her heart without asking anything in return, she had captured and enslaved him in a way that he knew was different from anything he had ever known or would ever know in the future.

It was not only her childlike belief and trust in him, it was also the vibrations between them that the Earl realised were unique and different from anything he had ever known with any other woman.

He was prepared to believe that they were two souls who had found one another again after a million lives and would go on into Eternity together.

He had so many things to explain to Cledra in the future.

But, as he looked down into her eyes brilliant with happiness with her lashes still wet from her tears, at her lips inviting his and at her face that seemed to have an unearthly radiance about it, he knew that he was the luckiest man in the whole world.

"What have you done to me, my precious, that I should feel like this?" he asked, "I was prepared to wager everything I possess that I should never feel so completely and helplessly in love."

"You are so wonderful," Cledra whispered. "I love you and there is nothing left in the whole world but my love – and I want to give it to you – and go on giving and giving – until I am – all yours."

The note of emotion in her voice told the Earl that he had awoken her to the first passionate desire that she had ever felt.

Because it was so alluring and at the same time so utterly innocent he knew that he must protect her not only against other men but against himself as well.

He would be very gentle because she was so young and so inexperienced.

He thought that of all the campaigns he had fought perhaps this would be the most intriguing and one which would require his instinct and perceptiveness together with his love that was so new to him to guide and inspire him.

He pulled her a little closer to him as he sighed,

"We have so much to give each other, my darling, now and in the future and I think the love we have found is not only something personal to ourselves but a victory over cruelty and evil."

"A Winged Victory," Cledra cried, "because when you kiss me and when you – touch me – you carry me on wings to a Heaven that is far more marvellous than anybody has ever been able to – describe it."

"That is just what I want you to feel," the Earl said, "and you are right, my precious little one, ours is a winged victory and we have won a battle where love has been overwhelmingly victorious."

Then he was kissing her again and there was only his arms, his lips and him, as he carried her up to the stars, where there was no fear, only LOVE.

OTHER BOOKS IN THIS SERIES

The Barbara Cartland Eternal Collection is the unique opportunity to collect all five hundred of the timeless beautiful romantic novels written by the world's most celebrated and enduring romantic author.

Named the Eternal Collection because Barbara's inspiring stories of pure love, just the same as love itself, the books will be published on the internet at the rate of four titles per month until all five hundred are available.

The Eternal Collection, classic pure romance available worldwide for all time.

Made in the USA
Coppell, TX
04 July 2021